ABSOLUTE KNOWLEDGE

Stories

ALSO BY IAN RANDALL WILSON

Hunger and Other Stories
Theme of the Parabola (poetry chapbook)
Out of the Arcadian Ghetto (fiction chapbook)
Great Things Are Coming (novella)

ABSOLUTE KNOWLEDGE

Stories

Ian Randall Wilson

Hollyridge Press
Venice, California

Hollyridge Press
P.O. Box 2872
Venice, California 90294

Cover Art © Photographer: Onion | Agency: Dreamstime.com
Author Photo, Cover and Design by Rio Smyth
Manufactured in the United States of America by Lightning Source

Publisher's Cataloging-In-Publication Data
(Prepared by The Donohue Group, Inc.)

Wilson, Ian Randall.
  Absolute knowledge : stories / Ian Randall Wilson.

  p. ; cm.

  ISBN-13: 978-0-9799588-2-3
  ISBN-10: 0-9799588-2-2

1. Short stories, American--21st century. I. Title.

PS3573.I456955 A62 2008
813/.6   2008931360

14 13 12 11 10 09 08   10 9 8 7 6 5 4 3 2 1

For Denise

Knowledge is ancient error reflecting on its youth.
——Francis Picabia, "Sayings"

Contents

Absolute Knowledge

HEGEL WAS WRONG, Max said to his mother, to his sister, to his track coach, to his literature Professor Salomon, to his girlfriend Julie, to anyone from a dwindling circle of those who would still listen. He didn't stop there. Art wasn't dead, he told Julie. Art flourished, it was Hegel who was gone. Religion wasn't the answer.

"Oh, Max," Julie said. "I liked you better when you were designing those pointy domes. At least that was a future. But this mind-body stuff. Let's go play house, Muffin."

Her eyes made artificially luminescent by blue contact lenses, crinkled at the sides. She licked her lips and smoothed back her blond ponytail, at the same time thrusting out her reasonable-sized, but less than full breasts. Max told her there was no time for playing house. "There's no time for playing house," he said. He had a mission. He was determined, following his graduation the next week, to begin his life's work: "I'm going to write The Book." She hadn't understood and he tried to explain it as a document which would be the artistic equivalent of Absolute Knowledge.

"Good night," said Professor Salomon, his face taking on a certain dubious expression when he heard the news. This was the expression he always took on when he was surprised or worried, though the contours of face were hidden by a full, black beard, and his eyes, made artificially luminescent by blue contact lenses, were lost in all that hair. His students often thought the Professor angry when he was actually smiling, Max among them. In spite of his doubts, some part of the Professor applauded this bold academic foray. "It's a bold academic foray," the Professor said. "I applaud it." He had never made any himself but Max was not up for tenure. The Professor also said, "I don't know if this will help your chances for a doctorate. Have you considered your father's business?"

Hours after the graduation ceremony, while the groundsmen picked up and bagged what would amount to 2.76 tons of mixed trash; while representatives of the gown rental company feverishly tried to gather in every fallen cap before the groundsmen threw them out as trash, so as to maximize gown rental profits and still claim the caps lost, allowing the rental company to keep the deposit; while other graduates went off to have seafood dinners trucked in from Maine with their parents and families; while others said good bye to favorite professors, the professors wishing they'd held out sexual favors for a higher grade knowing they yet had a chance to score in summer school; while still others walked around parts of the campus recalling the memory of the place they lost their virginity or smoked their first joint; and, while even more wished tearful farewells to people they'd hated all four years of school, and now for whom they felt such fondness; Max was already twenty miles down New Hampshire Route 93 heading for his parents' home in a suburb of Boston.

He moved in, reclaiming his old room. The shelves, filled with books, included an entire collection of *The Hardy Boys*, and the walls were covered with pendants and 19 pictures. Odd pictures from high school. His sister had taken them all prior to her discovery of the postmodern condition. She hadn't been as adept with her camera then as now, nor had her aesthetic underpinnings yet firmed, and so she had captured him in poses which highlighted the long hair and bushy sideburns but from eccentric angles with curious framing, chopping off a nose or a chin or half a face. He wore a crew cut now, easier to keep clean after long distance runs. In each picture, what portion of him visible, Max seemed to be staring quizzically at the lens as if asked a question he would never be able to answer at the precise moment the shutter snapped.

His parents kept silent about rent. "I hope his theory is going to provide for its own realization," his mother said to his father, their eyes, artificially luminescent by blue contact lenses, stared at one another.

"We won't be the ears for his mouth," said Max's father.

They weren't sure if they could resume asking him to mow the lawn or tend the flower beds or take out the trash.

"He'll have to realize that taking is not more blessed than giving," his father said.

"And that this isn't another Utopian exercise."

Max seemed too old to trade chores for some kind of allowance. His parents held quiet conferences in between commercial breaks of "The Tonight Show" and decided, finally, this was a phase.

"Revolution takes a long time to build its tents," his mother said.

"God is dead. Superman needs a job."

School had never been easy for Max and they thought a little rest might do him good. Still they enlisted Julie's support to push him along. She was losing patience quickly, though.

"Bite me, Muffin," she said to him on a Tuesday afternoon a few days after he came home. They were in his room. It was sunny and hot outside. A lawn sprinkler ran below. Julie wore a halter-top and held her bare shoulder for him to clamp onto.

"Don't you want to hear about my plans for chapter 2?" Max asked.

What was wrong with him? Max used to be such a decent lover, a little untutored perhaps, but vigorous. Now all he wanted to discuss was Hegel's place in the German Enlightenment.

There was no biting that afternoon nor a day later, when, mid-way through his discourse about the six levels revealed in the "Phenomenology" Julie shouted, "I don't care about level 4. I want to know when you're going to get a real job. I want to know when we're going to get married."

Max told her that marriage was out of the question until he moved the *Zeitgeist* to its proper place in society. Civilization demanded it. He was the one who could do it. She had to have faith. Julie repeated that world spirit was of no interest to her.

"When can we set the date?" she demanded.

Max went back to his lecture. His sister, her eyes made artificially luminescent by blue contact lenses which dramatically improved her vision, ducked in and fired off a few shots with her autofocus fast finder camera and strobe attachment. She was documenting the march to Absolute Knowledge. "Though if I take the pictures out of order," she said, "it obliterates the past."

"Are you trying to subvert me?" Max wanted to know.

Their father intimated it was going to be a march to Absolute Failure. Julie left the room, brushing past his sister, slamming the door. One of the 19 pictures dropped to the floor, the one capturing Max coming out of a pool, wet like a fat seal. That was all right. He was doing this for himself and if his audience deserted him he still needed to be clear on the concepts before he could hope to start on The Book.

He consulted his notes. "Level 4," Max began again.

In the first nine months of his work Max produced nothing. His sister, however, began to produce a body of work documenting his project.

"I may be able to distill you out of a grand narrative," she told him. "Besides, I love your right side."

She started each morning with a couple of tests shots of him then when on to shoot a whole roll of black and white. "The purity of your skin thrills me," she said. "What shadow!"

She promised to stay out of his way, paring down her lighting to one fill and one small key which operated on batteries. "A triumph of technology," she said.

Max smiled in the first few days as photographer and subject appeared to be in agreement, a misprision on his part.

"I'm not looking for consensus," his sister said. "I'm trying to make you at home in your alien being."

He looked thoughtful in the first few months as instability set in.

"Learn from Las Vegas," said his sister.

By the ninth month he looked worried in each picture. She showed him the proofs. The framing had improved dramatically. Now when his sister chopped off a body part it was for a good and well-considered artistic reason—part of her latent vision.

"Sometimes aesthetics functions as an unpleasant mirror," she said.

Such objectification unnerved him and began to undermine the very framework in which his previous normal science was conducted.

Also in the beginning, he bought a special journal with cream colored paper and a hand-tooled leather cover imported from Florence. But the book intimidated him. It was far too nice to write in so he put it in a drawer, choosing instead to lay out a small stack of white Xerox 4200DP 20LB paper, $5.99 a ream purchased at Spruce's Stationary Shop, 1521 Auburn Street, Auburndale, Massachusetts, one of the thirteen villages of Newton, Massachusetts, a mostly affluent suburb of Boston some eight miles from the financial district and the Old South Church. He also purchased a box of Associated 600 series Number 2 black lead pencils, $2.89 a dozen from the same store. These trips to the store were recorded dutifully on film by his sister who seemed never to tire of snapping away.

"Is all of this completely necessary?" Max asked.

"In the language game, these are your nodal points. I need to get them down if I'm going to get in on the exchange."

Julie objected to the attention but for different reasons: "You spend more time with her than me," she said. "I'd be happy to touch each and every one of your nodal points. Wouldn't you like that?"

Max demurred.

Julie said, "Maybe I should take up an art form. I could paint. I could document your march to absolute knowledge in a series of still lifes. You'd never know I was here."

"That's Absolute Knowledge, initial caps."

"Sorry."

"I'd know," said Max.

"Maybe I will," she said.

The stack of paper stayed pristine except for a brown ring where he put down his coffee cup. Max thought the ring significant though as yet he could not explain that significance. He decided not to throw the page away. The brown circle represented a smaller universe, a sort of subset of knowledge. After publication, reviewers and critics would point to its brilliant inclusion; no one would know that this was an accident about which he stayed upset for half a day. His sister recorded the spill, recorded his angry face framed by the door as he slammed it on her.

Max's mother noticed that the doors were slamming a good deal as the time passed. Max's father examined the frames and clucked that they'd have to replace the hardware if Max's current rate of transformation into the overman continued.

"It's not true that good intentions justify everything," his mother said.

"God is still dead," his father said. "Time to stop looking backward toward the dark ages."

Max sat in his old room most every morning, most every afternoon. Sometimes he wandered out on the property next door to his parents' corner lot, an old estate willed to the local junior college. The broad expanse of grass turned brown in places where the winter cold had frozen the ground. As children, Max and his friends sledded down the small hill in the middle of the property. He walked up the hill thinking, thinking, so intensely he failed to notice the slow circle of brown forming a warning track of dead pine needles at the base of an evergreen at the far end of the property. This was the goalpost marker for their fall football games. He walked into the tree, cutting himself. For the moment, thoughts of Hegel vanished, and his forehead hurt like hell.

On the morning of the twenty-second in this ninth month of work his day began like this: At 8 A.M. the alarm went off, a Sony combination clock radio received for his high school graduation and used for the last four years. On other mornings, he pushed the gray snooze button at least two, sometimes as many as four times depending upon what he ate for dinner the night before or whether he and Julie had fought, again. This morning it was three times.

The disc jockey announced the temperature at a brisk forty degrees. Then, while the traffic reporter described the choked conditions on the Southeast Expressway offering helpful advice on which exits to avoid, Max, moved from his prone position to a sitting one, where his elbows pressed on his knees, his chest hanging between, his head bent and dangling. This movement appeared to sap all his available energy and he stayed there through the end of the newscast into and beyond the next three songs, one of which was new, one of which he liked, one of which Julie liked. His eyes didn't focus and his mouth was cottony, his tongue thick. His hair pointed out in several different directions.

At last Max swiped at his face, yawned, stretched, groaned, then wavered between standing up and falling back into his bed.

"Max," his mother called, banging on the door, "time for blind decisions and painful commitments. Breakfast."

He lurched to his feet. He opened his door and stumbled out to the hallway, shuffling along the carpet, moving toward the bathroom. He bumped into the wall but didn't notice the impact. He wore boxer shorts now gray with age, the elastic top overstretched.

"The unit of information is the bit," his sister called, "and that's quite a bit you're showing me." She ran off a dozen shots with her new motor-drive and Zeiss zoom lens. "Who said we're in a crisis of representation," she told him as the camera automatically rewound.

Max sometimes stood in the mirror for half an hour looking at himself. This morning he hoped to see a muse sitting on his shoulder. He hoped to find a sign that would give him the word with which to start The Book. He hoped to find a sign that would give him any words that he might include in The Book. Nothing came and so he shaved and brushed his teeth, removed his shorts and sat down on the toilet. He had read all the magazines. There were no right words for his book here either. Just advice on keeping spice in your relationship from *Cosmo*, an article on building a combination bird feeder flower pot sundial wind-mill in *Popular Mechanics*, and a tale of real life heroics in *Reader's Digest*.

He flipped through the magazines staring at the ads, looking at pictures of women he would never meet, looking at pictures of products he would never need. The framing was wonderful, though not nearly as artistic as the pictures his sister took. He had to admit she had an eye though often she made him look a bit like a mad professor at work, his eyes leering, his body bent at the waist. The magazine ads demanded his attention, demanded his money that he didn't have, demanded recognition. Slowly he realized he was a refugee from a consumer society, and Julie was the biggest consumer of all.

Last night she managed to get him out of his room by promising she would do that "thing" he liked if he took a little drive. They ended up going to a jewelry store at the Newton Centre mall, arguing about wedding rings over frozen yogurts, and he drove home alone. He tried get to sleep but it was an hour before he fully relaxed.

Max showered and returned to his room where he dressed and sat at his desk for yet another half hour. Nothing came except his sister to photograph the nothingness. After she left, he played a little rhythm on the desktop, drumming with a pair of pencils. Nothing. He was about to start drawing but stopped himself. The page was supposed to represent Absolute Knowledge. He shouldn't despoil it with some mindless doodle.

But today his mind lagged and he began thinking what if Absolute Knowledge wasn't a construct of letters and words. They were only signifiers to begin with. They had no inherent meaning until attached to something else. Maybe drawing offered the answer. Besides, this was only a first draft. He'd retype.

Max drew a hangman's noose and placed a male character inside it. He put a chair under the victim's legs. He drew in a face and eyes. Then he wrote a short poem next to it: "how many grains of sand are absolutely necessary to fill up on empty hearts when the valves are all scattered, the only hope of restitution lies in sending out search parties early before the sun gets too hot forcing us to turn back when all the ice melts and smoke gets in our eyes?"

Who knows? Max wrote underneath.

He came downstairs and Julie was there. She told him she sorry for their argument last night. "Let's kiss and make up, Muffin," she said, "And never argue again."

Max smiled at her. His sister snapped away. His father folded the paper with a snap. "If you're going to the women," he said, "Don't forget the whip." His mother poured coffee. Outside, a car honked. Mail dropped through the slot. The screen door slammed. The toast popped up.

"How's the work this morning?" Julie asked.

He told her he had written a poem about genius and talent and that, linked with multi-cultural drawings, this might represent a new critical beginning for him.

"And Zarathustra was just sighted in Hollywood," his father said snapping the newspaper. "Pass the toast."

"Now Harold, history is strange object," Max's mother chided.

The camera ran off more pictures. Max's sister moved around the table catching Max with a bit of toast around his mouth, Julie staring at Max and licking her lips, Max's mother with her head bowed and Max's father, his lips pursed in a sour expression.

"Harold nothing," Max's father said. "There are no overmen at this table. I want the toast."

"Professor Salomon said it might help in my dissertation."

"More school?" Julie and Max's parents said together.

"Pass the toast," Max said.

Day 331. Nothing.
Day 366. Nothing.

Day 412. Nothing.

Day 471. Nothing. Nothing. Nothing.

But his sister's photo collection grew. "Society is a giant machine and I'm one of its little motors," she said. "Or I'm going to be when I'm done with you."

The first page was covered with doodles now, an entire family being hung, another of a man looking remarkably like Professor Salomon torching a pile of books on which was tied a younger man who looked like Max. The center of the coffee ring was open. Max moved on to a second page.

More than a year before, when he started, he kept his window open. He liked to hear the sounds of cars passing by the side street that abutted his parents' home. It was a rough road that bordered his house and the estate of the junior college. Cars bumped along, tires spraying gravel and engines working harder. He like to hear the birds that settled in the trees out back singing as the sun went down. He liked to watch the progress of the life as the sun reached its zenith then descended, the shadows lengthening, the golden light dropping lower and lower on the wall, the air damping down and a feeling coming that the day was ending. Now he kept it closed, the shades pulled. Any outside distraction was too much for him. This task was too much for him. He wanted to be outside running and laughing and listening to the those birds.

His father moved beyond discussions on the death to God to an explanation of the finite boundaries of energy in the universe, to the nature of energy conservation, and the possibility of eternal change—and eternal recurrence.

"He could just ask me to get a job," Max said, hearing arguments muffled and distant from his parents' bedroom. They no longer waited for commercial breaks but argued right through Johnny's monologue and into the interview of the first guest.

He wasn't lazy. He worked hard every day. He wasn't stupid. He graduated at the middle of his class. He may have been a waste of money but if he succeeded, honor, glory, and unlimited money would flow in. He had already determined that his parents would share.

But Julie...

They had not made love in nine weeks and he was beginning to see her less and less.

"I'm busy," was all she said.

No, I'm busy, Muffin, or of course I'm thinking about you, Muffin, or how is your work coming, Muffin? or when can you show me something, Muffin? And certainly no, I love you, Muffin. She didn't get it.

The other blow was his rejection for the doctoral program under Professor Salomon. The professor offered his condolences. He understood how the quest to find the artistic equivalent of Absolute Knowledge was a difficult one, fraught with peril. Certainly, if things got better, space might be found at a later date. "Keep plugging," Professor Salomon said, then reminded Max there was still time to investigate his father's line of work.

He started taking breaks to clear his head. During one of those breaks, Max visited an eye doctor. He thought about being fitted for blue contact lenses but decided against it: They made his eyes seem too luminescent.

Max also started running to escape. He didn't have to think about anything except the route, his stride length, his next breath. His pounding steps carried him past the new buildings thrown up on concrete slabs; past the iron fence of a girl he knew as a child, her name forgotten, where they looked into each other eyes as little kindergarten children and said, I love you, though neither of them knew what it meant; past the lawns of another friend's house where the kids had played tag football games that always got too rough; past the golf course that barred anyone who couldn't trace their heritage back in a direct line to one of the original passengers on the Mayflower—being related to a crew member didn't count.

He ran through old neighborhoods with houses dating back to the last century, past trees even older. He ran on the paths that used to take him to Williams Elementary School, Warren Junior High School and beyond. He raced the subway. He raced commuters on their way home. He ran up and down land formations carved out by the movements of glaciers millions of years before.

There was a secret here in the cycle of his breathing. His pulse. He caught the tip of it but then it got away. Somewhere in the fifth mile he thought about when he was 16 and took the car, invited to some party. He and his friend Gary. They hadn't talked in years. That night they stopped at another friend's house who was grinding pot in a blender. Brown dust settled around the blades and sticks crackled. They smoked from a piece of foil rolled and burned black. Max took his turn, held the smoke until his eyes watered and his throat burned, until he had to blow it out or pass out or fly or never breathe again. In the next moment he was sure wires were coming out of the wall, windows snapping in martial time as the carpet bled pebbles over the door. His mother warned him that knowledge and action were two poles of a single existence—and not to drink and drive.

Outside, dark words blurred into theories: *He would die from too much presuming on his heart, erasing the lines from his face. He would cry without eyes.* Ten minutes later he was still throwing up. He had to let Gary drive. He had to let Gary explain. He leaned back, forced his eyes closed, tried to rest it off, to stop the floor from spinning, to get up some wet in his mouth. He prayed to the usual suspects not to let his parents know. He prayed to a few others: Maurice Merleau-Ponty, Jean-

François Lyotard, Friedrich Nietzsche—promising he would never let this happen again. He would never drink. He would never smoke. He would lead a retiring life.

He ran and breathed and moved with the light as the sun went down and the wind came up. He ran and he breathed and moved with the dark as the night dissolved the trees into shadows and the houses started to pale.

His sister drove by, leaning out the window, shooting pictures. "Keep going, Max," she called. "Don't deny us the solace of good forms. Think of this as part of a cyclical moment—"

"A what?"

"Cyclical movement that returns before the emergence of an ever newer modernism. We're catching the wave."

Why was the story of the bad dope and the hallucinations coming to him? His wave? It had something to do with being and nothingness, the weightless feeling he remembered sitting in that chair stoned out of his mind. Each time he ran he conjured up the story and tried to remember the wildness of his thoughts on that night. Wires and walls and martial music, windows snapping in time to the beat. Gary explaining. He didn't know. Sweat drenched his white shirt turning it gray. He panted. His lungs burned. His father pointed at him and said, "Another example of mankind continuing to surpass itself."

❧•❧

He was three days away from two years of nothing. He had covered six sheets with drawings and poems on the order of: "when dice roll nothing stops chance" or "lace, thinking itself lace, is not lace as soon as it thinks." His sister had submitted a portion of her portfolio and won a national photo competition. A story on her was the featured piece of this month's *Photo*

Magazine. She got a thousand dollars and three calls from photo reps, one of whom was the biggest in New York City. She used a portion of her money to buy Max a new cushion for his chair. "In this search for new presentations, I want you to be comfortable," she said. "We may be in this a long time."

"What do you think of my project," Max wanted to know.

"I think you're stuck in the last century, Max," she said. "*Bildung* and knowledge have split. You have to find a way to bring it to the market. We're all trading commodities, my man, these pictures are my little slice of heaven's bottom line. A little to the right, okay?"

Julie had vanished. She no longer stopped by. She didn't return calls. She failed to write back to the fifteen letters he sent, nor did she respond to the entire collection of Hallmark "I Love You and I'm Thinking Of You" card series he purchased on sale at Spruce's Stationary Shop. Mr. Spruce felt bad for him and offered him a job in the stock room. "Just for spending money," he said.

Professor Salomon had moved on as well. He was on sabbatical in Paris hoping to make a connection between the work of the French Reconstructionists—a new literary movement not widely known anywhere except for a long block of the 14th *Arondisement*—and an equally little known text written by Proust's idiot savant cousin, Reme.

Max was in despair. He drew a circle and colored it in. He drew squares, triangles, rectangles, pentagrams, parallelograms, hexagrams, decigrams, octahedrons, tetrahedrons. He used up every Greek designation he knew. He wrote down random words. The words of his favorite novel. The words of songs he loved. The words of songs he hated. The words of songs Julie hated.

Max was in despair and ready to give up.

The door burst open, banging against the wall, sending two more of the 19 high school pictures onto the floor. It was Julie, out of breath looking at him, hard. For once, Max's sister was no where to be seen. Julie's hair was cut short and she was not as thin as he remembered her. Her jaw was thrust out and he thought her a bit manly in boots and denim overalls.

"All right," she said. "I've had enough. I tried to be supportive. That didn't work. I tried to trick you into giving me a ring. That didn't work. I tried to play hard to get and that didn't work. I even tried to ignore you and that didn't work the worst of all."

She was carrying a knapsack on her back and she slammed it onto his desk sending the papers flying.

"Hey," said Max. "My work. My work."

"Forget about that, Muffin. We have to talk. I've spent the last nine months studying this stuff day and night. Day and night, do you hear me? I've read Hegel, Heserl, Heidigger and ever other god damn German Enlightenment philosopher that begins with an H. I've read the New Criticism, the Old Criticism. And then I even read Derrida—in French. And I've got the answer. I've figured it out. You're right. Hegel was wrong. But not for the reasons you think. Here it is."

She drew a series of steps, explained the shifting nature of absolutes, about Hegel's own pretentiousness that allowed him to declare things are the way they are because he said so, and certain French Existentialists that acknowledged the unavoidable intrusion of the historian into history.

"It's a restatement of uncertainty," she said.

"I know all this," said Max.

"But that's why the answer isn't in the west—all that nostalgia for the unattainable," she said, "it's in east. Nargarjuna said, 'Whatever is dependently co-arisen that is explained to be emptiness.' He's saying there's not independent existence. Absolute

Knowledge is impossible. Everything depends upon conventions, the way you define things."

Her eyes were a different color. She'd given up the blue contact lenses for something, other.

"Look," she said, "some people wonder why I love you. I've wondered it too. But it's the way my system is defined. Me relative to you produces love. Sappy, but that's the way I am. There's nothing to stop history. Because Hegel said so? Because you say so? Nothing. Only the end of time and we're a long way from that, Muffin."

In a sweep, she pushed the books off the desk where they joined the rest of the papers on the floor. She reached behind her and flipped the door shut. Then she tore Max shirt off.

All he could think as Julie began licking his neck was, You know, she just might be right. Outside, children from the junior college preschool laughed and shouted. Cars drove by. The sun went down. Max and Julie made love.

Three Strikes People

PRISON MIGHT BE HIS LAST best hope, and Pelican Bay—from some reports the most brutal in the California penal system—had the highest rate of acceptance in the Best All-US Poetry Anthology for the last three years in a row. Pelican Bay had the highest number of appearances in ten of the most important literary journals in the country including *The Paris Review*, *Grand Street*, and *The New Republic*. Pelican Bay had gotten more poets their first published volume of poetry than any MFA program anywhere on the planet.

These days it seemed impossible to get published through normal channels. After logging in another batch of rejections, which brought the year's total rejections to 475, Josh sat reading one Saturday a couple of weeks before Christmas. In several Best All-US Poetry anthologies he noticed a trend: In 1994 poems from three prison inmates appeared. In 1995 the anthology published poems from a dozen. By 1996, 75% of the volume came from men and women serving time. All had multiple publications elsewhere. Josh hadn't had a poem accepted in two years, couldn't get beyond the first round of any literary contest.

"Aren't you always saying it's the work that matters, not publication?" Christina, his girlfriend said that night.

"I may be the most obscure poet in America."

"I'm sure there are more obscure."

The 1997 editor made introductory remarks about the importance of political poetry: The best new voices were to be found not on college campuses nor in coffee houses, nor from white men of a certain age or older. Unit 12 of the Security Housing Units at Pelican Bay in California seemed unusually fertile ground. Of the poems in the volume, half were from Pelican Bay inmates.

"I may *always* be the most obscure poet in America."

"Isn't that where the worst of the worst go?"

"If something doesn't change."

They were supposed to go to a film but Christina arrived late; she was always working. They ended up going for a walk. At the beginning of their relationship she said she admired him for taking a subsistence job so he'd have time to write. But he never made enough money to take her out to the kind of restaurants her friends dined in nor on vacations somewhere other than free museums. He knew, and he felt badly. In two and half years of going out they made no progress toward marriage, family or the purchase of a home. How could he without an established career? She'd started to apply her own pressure, suggesting he try screenplays. "For the money," she said, and then he could write whatever it was he wanted to write. "Well it doesn't have to be screenplays, that's just the quickest way. You could do anything and keep writing on the side. Think of Williams. Think of Stevens." Though she was a studio script reader, she'd been a lit major in school and knew the names.

"Doctor, lawyer, and me, the typist. I don't think I'm working up to my potential."

"No one is disagreeing."

"No one seems to be hearing me," Josh said, "I'm writing into the void. 'Writing into the void,' hey, that's not a bad start. Can I borrow a piece of paper?"

"I read about that Pelican Bay place," his weight trainer said the next day. Josh allowed himself the luxury of workouts, and by pre-paying a full year in advance he got a great rate. The trainer said: "Elbows in. What did I read?—You're alone for 23 hours a day. Breathe. When you're taken for exercise they put you in chains—two, three, keep going—and you're ordered to look at the floor. No talking. Eight. Good. The cells are always under surveillance. Give me two more. Sounds like a real fun place."

"I think that's in some of the security units," Josh said before his next set of bench press. "But not all. The rest of the place isn't so bad."

"What's your conception of *bad*, Josh?" a class member asked him after the last workshop of the semester. "That was a nice image in line three by the way but I still disagree with your breaks. I've been in jail. County."

"You always disagree with my breaks," Josh said.

"Got my head banged up and bloody and spent the night lying in my own piss. Power to the people, my ass."

An idea was forming, and he brought it up again to Christina. As fast as MFA programs grew—and there were now some 400—prison poetry programs grew faster as more prisons were built than schools. Josh, working on his own, got nowhere. He needed a new approach. In the time before the end of the year he made ten submissions a day and got back the same number. The submissions had been opened, a form rejection added to the bundle, and the whole mess inserted back in the SASE. They looked as if they hadn't been read, cover letters still attached—a conclusion confirmed by one form response which read: *We don't accept unsolicited fiction but if you'd like to send us poetry, we'll consider it.* Bastards.

Every prison, he told Christina, instituted a writing program as they cut back on everything else.

"Is this some metaphor you're working out against marriage?" she asked.

A few pads of paper, some pencils whose use was strictly monitored, a privilege to be given out or revoked.

"Poetry calmed down the participants," he said.

"Poetry is beginning to upset *me*," Christina said.

"Cheaper than drugs. Cheaper than solitary."

Poetry didn't make them docile but let them express feelings, the Aristotelian catharsis. Instead of lifting weights inmates wrote sonnets, were introduced to the rudiments of the villanelle, led on to writing free verse. The more that got published the better they felt, no doubt.

"No doubt," said Christina.

"Have you ever wondered," Josh said, "what it would take to land in prison, to get into one of the programs?"

"If you want to stop going out," Christina said, "you could just say so."

The turnaround on his submissions was so fast. He got ten more rejections in the same condition the next day. He might as well have been writing to himself, for himself—and that one about unsolicited fiction: bastards.

"Think of it," he told her, "as a way to a career."

"I don't want to."

Crime or its report and aftermath was all around him and he'd never noticed. The closest he'd gotten to law enforcement was a debate with a meter maid who wrote him a ticket just after the meter flipped. She was sorry but she'd already started. Driving home from school one night after the semester began, traffic vanished on the other side of the Santa Monica Freeway. Just past the West LA interchange a man knelt by the side of the road, a man with dark skin and his hands behind his head, fingers interlaced. Five police cars with their lights flashing parked a hundred feet away. What had he done? Why had he run? Ten officers approached in a combat crouches, guns drawn, shouting.

Two mornings later Josh got on the freeway hoping this alternative might be a faster way to work, but traffic backed up for at least half a mile. Cars traveled ten feet forward then stopped.

Josh changed radio stations, adjusted his shirt, his shoulder belt, tapped the steering wheel in time to the music. A sheriff's bus pulled beside him—black and white with mesh and bars across the window and a sign announcing prisoner transport. No faces were visible through the windows though once when Josh came up even with the bus's front he saw a deputy in mirrored aviator sunglasses facing back toward the interior of the bus holding a shotgun. The deputy had a booted foot against a divider.

Terse items appeared in the paper: *Robbery at City Bank, Braddock and North; suspect, one Hispanic male, 20s, approximately six feet, carried off $10,000 after shooting guard.* He drove by the scene: At one door yellow police tape flapped in the breeze, the bank closed indefinitely.

Burglary attempted at private residence at 14 Silver Strand. Alarm triggered and suspects fled scene. Burglary at 26 Silver Strand. Suspects broke in through rear glass patio door. Jewelry and three paintings taken. Just a residential street, no remnants of the crime. Cars parked along the sidewalk. A man walking his dog. Two runners sauntered by. Josh didn't stop to park.

A 1994 Cadillac Seville stolen outside LeMere's Liquor Store. No witnesses. Business was brisk as the Lottery ran over 20 million and the lot filled and emptied twenty times an hour in a constant turn-over of cars. Some broken glass was the only reminder of the theft, but that might have come from a bottle dropped in an inebriated lurching toward a car door. As if the crime had never occurred. The victim knew, left to deal with police reports, insurance companies, car rental agencies. But the world went on. It reminded Josh of reading poetry in public. For a moment, you held the audience, and then the night was over.

That evening on the news an arraignment of the "bird-caller rapist," a man who warbled like a whitebeam during his assaults. The prisoner, led in through a side door, stood before a waist-high wooden wall. He shuffled along in leg irons and chains wrapped around his waist that secured his hands to his belt. He wore a bright red jumpsuit with black letters stenciled across his back. There were other prisoners in the pen behind waiting for their arraignment.

⁕•⁖

In workshop, his poems began to feature a criminal thematic. *A man stabs his brother*, one of his new poems began. "Are you going Biblical on us now, Josh?" the professor asked during the criticism phase. Other class members complained that the work didn't seem authentic, the language flat, the ideas too didactic.

"But crime is part of the landscape," Josh said.

"Pick a different tree," a class member said.

In prison they had showers once a week, three meals a day, a place to sleep. Incarceration for publication. Incarceration for publication. Could he handle life in prison? Josh was 6'2" and 225. Conscious of diet, exercising frequently, he was muscular. A cable program on prisons claimed that new inmates, their first night or so, had their front teeth broken by other inmates in order to facilitate oral sex. Forced sodomy was a problem. Josh increased his workouts, lifted heavier weights. He began kick-boxing several times a week at his gym. He had a naturally strong left hook and was developing an excellent front snap-kick.

"You could hurt someone," the instructor said.

"I'm a poet," Josh told him.

His body frequently sore, he slept more. Christina complained about a lack of love-making.

"We're sticking with the national average," Josh said.

One Saturday morning Josh suggested to Christina they take a drive. He needed research for a "new project" whose subject she didn't question. They headed off northeast to the desert, not talking much, traversing freeways with the windows down, playing music. As they passed through a stretch of road that had been blasted out of sand-colored mountains, Christina said, "It's pretty country out here, but a little bleak. We haven't done much of this lately."

Josh told her, "Do you know that on the four-hundred-miles between Sacramento and Los Angeles, you're never more than about forty minutes away from a state prison. They've got great names: Folsom, Vacaville, Mule Creek, Stockton, Tracy, Chowchilla, Coalinga, Avenal, Corcoran, Delano, Wasco, Tehachapi, Lancaster."

Christina looked at him but said nothing.

A half hour later they were in Lancaster. Josh consulted a slip of paper and made several turns off the freeway exit. "There it is," he said.

The facility was marked by discreet signs that pointed the way to what looked like a factory or a bleak high school, one surrounded by razor wire and an electric fence with guard towers ringing the perimeter.

"There's what?" Christina asked.

"Home. Well it could be my new home. I have to start somewhere. I wanted to see what it looked like."

Christina said nothing on the way back. She declined his offer of dinner and was out of the car before he had stopped it. Josh didn't hear from her for a week.

During that time he studied the California Penal Code. Once you were convicted, the Department of Corrections used a point system numbered I-IV to determine custody level and how restrictive your environment would be. A prisoner got two points for being below age 26, two for not completing high school, two for being unmarried, two for not having been in the military, and up to twelve points for having prior offenses. A prisoner also got points equal to the number of years of his sentence multiplied by three. The points were added up and the total corresponded to a security level: 52 points and above got you Level IV, maximum security.

The Pelican Bay program was in the maximum security part of the prison. Without prior offenses, Josh could count on only four points—two for not being married and two for not being in the military. That meant he had to make up the rest with his sentence length. He needed 16 years but also the possibility of parole so that once his career was established, he could get out and reap the benefits.

He ruled out murder, kidnapping, rape and other sex crimes, crimes against minors, and crimes against the elderly over 65. No one should get hurt for the sake of poetry. No reason to make his stay more difficult, and he needed a forgivable offense, one for which he could believably repent—when he got out.

Theft of a gun would get him three years. Conversion of an assault weapon to fully-automatic, three years. Possession of a machine gun, one year. Car theft, one year.

Sixteen years was a tough sentence to get without hurting someone. One scenario had him steal a handgun and a machine-gun and a car, buy an assault weapon and convert it to fully automatic, then end up on a school grounds—a middle-school so the police would take him seriously but not be as worried that he was going to gun down babies—in session in possession of all the firearms, all of them loaded. Caught on school grounds with the weapons would get him seven years. If a judge didn't sentence him concurrently for all of these offenses, he would end up with the necessary time—and Pelican Bay.

Josh came home from class one night and found Christina waiting. Dressed in a man's flannel shirt and jeans, she sat on the stoop and smoked a thin black cigarette.

"When did you take those up again?" he said.

"I lost my key," she told him.

"Did we have plans? I would have come home sooner."

"Do you know that's the fourth one I've lost."

She ground her cigarette into the dirt beside six others, pulled an open pack from her shirt pocket and shook one out. Lighting it with a disposable lighter, she took a big drag then blew the smoke out in a rush.

"The fourth one," she said. "Do you think I have a problem with commitment?"

"I'll give you another key."

She took a big drag and another, stubbed the cigarette out and lit one more.

"I don't want to go in," she said.

He sat next to her and said, "We had a great class tonight. My new sestina was well received."

"Yes," she said, and waved the cigarette around to punctuate her words. "I bet you had every one in chains. They were bound up over the formal structure. You had them doing time with your line breaks."

"Don't I at least get a kiss," he said.

"Your metaphors were in shackles. I have more. You gave them a chain-gang of imagery. No one was paroled from commenting on the—"

"I had a good poem. Another good one. Everyone said."

"Did you know they're cutting back on conjugal visits?"

"Did you read that in a script?"

"What will we tell our children? 'Daddy's finally a successful poet but he's serving 25 to life.'"

"That's only for three strikes people. I was thinking of something lower level."

"Grand theft auto? Larceny? Armed robbery? How about rape. I could help out on that one."

"Rapists get the hardest time next to child molesters."

"If you keep this going you're going to kill me and then you *will* be doing 25 to life, but I won't be around."

She flicked the cigarette down the walkway where it bounced along the concrete scattering red embers, coming to rest on the edge of a pool of light from an overhead bulb.

"I won't be the first poet who's gone to jail, you know," he said, "poetry requires sacrifices. All art does."

"Don't do this," she said.

"I can't stay unknown."

Smoke from the dead butt curled upward in a gyre vanishing in the black sky.

After she left Josh found himself evaluating his life. What do poets make? To the popular culture a poet was a dreamer, more sensitive than other people, unafraid to show feeling. And he did, he shared. Friends in *The Business* applauded Josh's "hobby." They wished they too had an outside pursuit. Some of them turned to boxing. Others went to classes at the UCLA Extension, to open their minds, they said, to see something beyond these god damn movies.

Would he teach?—the most frequent question. Would he give up his job for a PH.D.? Was he a perpetual student? Eternal student? How many degrees did he need?

Hemingway didn't stay in college, someone volunteered.

Hemingway wrote horrible poetry, Josh said.

Novelists have worlds to create. The best, Gass said, came to believe in invisible beings, gods and angels, wills and powers, atoms, voids. Josh wanted a lasting image, a single image, recognized at the bone level. Something more than a red wheel barrow or an old man in a dry month or a spot of time. So much history he was not a part of.

The good men have all been taken, a secretary lamented.

So have all the good images, Josh told her.

He wanted recognition, publication, limited fame. He was, after all, a poet, not a rock star. In the morning ten more rejections. The morning after, another ten. No notes. Silence—from out there.

He went back to LeMere's and parked across the street. A crime where no one would be hurt including himself. The building sat on a lot at the intersection of two streets. He wasn't going to be shot dead in the commission of an armed robbery. No poetry in an early death, Keats the exception. A crime against property. Customers passed in and out of the store from a sizable parking lot. A car could be stolen in a quick move with a jimmy slid down in between the glass and frame of the driver's side window. That's how they did it on TV. The thief acted decisively, as if he belonged. Walk to the car, a quick look around, then, in the pause between customers, the thief slipped the lock, got inside and broke the ignition with another tool.

Where did car thieves get their equipment? There was no car thief store. But he was wrong about that. On the internet he found a company supplying those exact goods. They tailored their pitch to the repo business, locksmiths and tow-truck drivers. Vin's House of Tools in Lawrence, Kansas provided detailed instructions with each purchase. For orders over $50 the customer got a free Vin's t-shirt, and for orders over $100 a Vin's sweatshirt and key-ring.

With the ignition lock broken, the car had only to be hot-wired. A pro could do it in twenty seconds, an internet article proclaimed. Josh ordered the tools and practiced on his own car. He became proficient at slipping the lock. The ignition broke with surprising ease.

"What's wrong with the car," Christina asked when they saw each other again. She was giving them another chance.

Josh told her someone had tried to steal it. "I haven't had the chance to get it fixed."

"So now you hot-wire your own car?"

"I'm getting good at it. I'm down to thirty seconds. The pros are faster though," Josh said.

"Take me home," Christina told him.

He went back to LeMere's but felt too exposed. What about a larger location, one at the mall parking lots whose size assured anonymity? But patrols had been stepped up. Attempted theft wouldn't do. Without a record and as a first offender he'd be back on the street with probation.

He made a decision: He would steal a car from a local street and then be caught next to a school possessing a sizable quantity of drugs—there were plenty of schools in his neighborhood. But no guns to minimize the possibility of physical harm. A high speed chase would help.

He got his things in order. First he quit his job, surprising everyone. He could live for a month without income. His immediate superior and the department head tried to talk him out of it. They told him he was needed. He did too good a job for them to let him get away. Perhaps they could get him more money, a promotion, an assistant.

Josh declined. He needed a change. Then he emptied his apartment of its furnishings in a series of sidewalk sales, sold off his clothing except for one suit and tie, a dress shirt and a pair of dress shoes, three t-shirts including the one from Vin's, two pairs of jeans, a pair of running shoes and enough underwear and socks to last a week. He sold his appliances, his television, his pots and pans, his silverware, his stereo and his bed. He kept a small card table for the computer, one chair, and his telephone. He boxed up all his books and sent them to his parents in Boston with a request that they hold them in the garage along with the rest of the things they'd stored for him over the years. He rented a safe deposit box, paying for 50 years in advance, storing the few valuables he had plus disk and paper copies of all of his poems. The apartment was as empty as if no one had ever lived there. He ate on paper plates, brought in take-out pizza or Chinese food.

The money he made gave him enough to buy 14 grams of cocaine, two ounces of marijuana, and a half dozen packets of heroine. This quantity of drugs would put him in the "sell, furnish, give transport" category of the Health & Safety Code, and would up the prison time.

All of these preparations took two weeks. He thought of writing a note to Christina—who seemed not to be talking to him—but the prosecutor might try to introduce it as evidence that would keep him out of prison.

He went to his safe deposit box and dropped off the last of his new poems and disks. He packed the rest of his clothing in a box marked for Christina, and put the computer in there too. He stacked her gift boxes next to the door. In the rush of the Christmas season and her withdrawal from the relationship, they'd never exchanged presents.

At 10 P.M. on a Tuesday night, three weeks after quitting his job, he shut out the lights of his apartment, checked and rechecked faucets, burners and ovens as if making preparations for an extended vacation.

He called Christina and left a message on her machine saying that he hoped she understood, that he loved her and that he hoped he'd see her soon. He wrapped the cocaine and the other drugs in a plastic baggy and put it inside an inner pocket. Then he put the jimmy up his sleeve, the tool for breaking the ignition lock in his jacket pocket. Before he went out the door, he phoned the police. "It looks like there's someone breaking into a car at 14th and Idaho," he said. "Hurry."

Indivisible

THEY HAVE CAUGHT ME, at last, tonight, the story threatens to come to an end. It began in 1950, days after my graduation from Dartmouth College. I was, then, a proper student, a good student, morally pure and disciplined in my habits. I rose every morning before seven to perform a few minutes of rough calisthenics; that, too, is a lifetime habit. I changed toothbrushes promptly every three months though concerns about tooth decay were not so pronounced then as they are now. I held a bachelor's degree in Mathematics, and professed an unusually strong desire to make my mark on the world of science. Now, I am approaching sixty as surely as the numbers I count reel ahead. The next prime number—my so far elusive goal—waits for me.

I began my search for the next prime number in the beginning of the summer of that year so long ago. Truman was still president. My father, a war veteran, was back to work. An infestation of boring caterpillars destroyed the best vegetation behind my parents' house; the trees never recovered. It was fifteen years before we again had dense foliage. I never actually saw the green return, I heard about it from my mother.

The first numbers came fast and easily: 1, 3, 5, 7, 11. Anyone can do it by memory. Children learn of this early in school, name a number which can not be divided by any other except itself. Then, there were only simple adding machines available, certainly none of the computers that my sister told me of years later. She has urged me so many times since my parents' death to let her bring one in, to let the machine help me in my task. But I always refuse. There is something about machines and all those electrons whirling that sullies the process. The only true count can be found by searching in the mind. None of the great discoveries came about by computer. Did Gallileo define our universe with a computer? Did Newton codify the third law of thermodynamics with a computer? Or Einstein and his theory of relativity? None of them did and neither shall I. My goal then is my goal now: I am in my bedroom, a modest room a hundred feet square with a bed and a desk and reams and reams of paper covering the floor. I will remain in my room until I find the next prime number.

My parents were at first happy to have me home with them again. My mother, in particular, fluttered about preparing pot roasts every third night. At the time no link had been established between aggression and red meat, between heart disease and saturated fats. They were pleased by my diploma and the achievement it signified. My father finished high school but went no further in his studies and my mother—because of her place in her family—not even that. They gladly returned my childhood bedroom to me and thought nothing of my taking down the pendants, putting away the trophies for track. I won several in cross-country running; I was a long-distance man. They thought nothing of my taking down of the bookshelves, thought nothing of my moving the armoire into the garage. My father briefly questioned this last move, but I explained I needed the room.

The count began with the number 1. How very fitting. Then 3, quickly past 7, 11, 13, past 17, 19, 23, the numbers accumulated and I sprang into the hundreds, moving higher and higher as if I were climbing a tall peak whose upper reaches vanished into the clouds.

After the initial novelty of my presence dissipated, my father became concerned about my livelihood. He came to my door and asked me how long did I plan to sit at my desk counting? I had just completed a difficult calculation and calculated there was enough time to speak to him then. He understood the concept of the prime number but did not realize its value. I patiently explained that the goal of finding the next prime number was important in and of itself and would be its own form of gratification. He asked if the next prime number would pay the rent, buy food, convince a young woman that I was stable enough to marry. How different we were, he and I. This was to be my crusade. But, to settle his concerns, I told him that in the world of science and academia, the discovery of the next prime number was sure to bring me a prestigious appointment and sufficient income to live as I might need.

At first, I took my meals with the family, though I kept my time with them short. My girlfriend was understanding. She had waited for me through college, she waited for me now. She took to joining us for dinners and then walking me back to my room so I could begin my night counting. Her perfume lingered with me as did the clutch her moist hand in mine, her quick kiss at the corner of my mouth. I put a stop to these walks to my room. They were too distracting. It became too hard to keep count. I found myself wandering to the window and looking out over the street where I played as a boy. We built forts on this street, elaborate affairs of snow and ice, and conducted our own bombardments using principles the Romans had discovered when waging war on Carthage. All the original trees were there though stripped of their vegetation, but many of the boys had gone, moved to other cities or lost to the war. I got an occasional bit of news at lunch. My mother might point to a story in the paper, sometimes a picture of one of them was featured.

Even thinking of my girlfriend interfered with my work and, as she could not see how important my counting was, I began to limit my contact with her to once a week. I don't believe we ever discussed it but eventually, she stopped coming to dinner. My mother made some reference to a trip to Europe, a romance in Paris. Marriage. I forget exactly when this happened.

On about the fourth year of my counting, I passed by the prime number 1,163,143. This was real progress. To celebrate, my father invested in a television. He tried to get me to watch some with him after dinner—game shows where huge amounts of money were at stake. The questions never interested me and they avoided math. Young men, my age, sweating under the glare of bright lights; none of it mattered, and I saw what an even greater distraction this bulky contrivance with its wood sides and thickly curved glass front would be. After that, I took my meals in my room, taped the curtains shut, and only came out to shower and use the bathroom.

I was not entirely cut off. I heard about the killing of the young president, the civil rights marches, the rioting, the losses in Vietnam, the walk on the moon, the fall of another president. This news of the world came sometimes from my mother, but mostly from my sister who seemed to relish bringing me my tray. She had to step carefully around the piles of folded papers, the wadded up papers, the bags filled with papers. I had a unique filing system and I was never through with anything; I might need information on any of these sheets at any time. My parents feared for my health, and my sister suggested that I could do with some newer, cleaner clothes, but I asked her to assure them that I was fine, that my old things were fine, and that the task was important.

I was not entirely cut off, and my life—to me—was pleasant, though a struggle, because the work was so difficult. I wanted for nothing, I missed nothing. It was all right for former friends, for contemporaries to tour Europe, raise a family, found careers. That was for them but I had chosen a goal, a mission far more pure and holy.

In the fifteenth year I counted through to the prime number 19,009,989, and my father died leaving a modest inheritance. My mother insisted I attend his service, come with them to the grave. I did so from a measure of respect. In the month before he died my father spent a great deal of his time on a chair on the lawn beneath my window. I saw him once when the tape closing the curtains let loose. He waved and I nodded. He was the kind of man who talked about the changing season and explained how one day I would understand sleet as the last manifestation of denial as if in this I might gather some vague notion of myself. I never understood why I was his son—and then he was gone.

The count went on. All the answers were in the numbers. My room filled with paper stacked on every inch of carpet and every available surface. I filled the closets with paper. I had to ask my sister to store some in the basement for me as well. She complained of the musty smell but I convinced here that it was only a residual odor from the manufacturing process; nothing to worry about.

In the twenty-fifth year I hit the number 163,163,159. I was so far along. So far. The numbers stretched behind me in an unbroken chain of past memory. They were a link to my youth.

Still I counted and my mother passed away. That was a loss. She seemed to support me though in the months before her death I had little, if any contact with her though I traced her presence by following the scratch of her broom down the hall. I believed she stayed away to allow me my concentration because she knew how important my work was to the world, not only to me. In this way I measured her devotion.

Sometimes I thought I had it. In the thirty-seventh year I was almost sure. My God, what a sense of elation came to me. The prime number, the next prime number was mine. But a careful check and recheck revealed a flaw in my calculations. I had mistaken a five for a six. An honest mistake, a fault of poor hand-writing and a too-blunt pencil, but it set me back. At first it depressed me to the point that I stopped work for a half a day. I sat at my desk with my hands folded in my lap and I tried to conjure up scenes from my past. Hanover was a thriving town, so I heard, and my school had added on many new buildings, my old schoolmates, the benefactors.

I saw my sister grow worried. I saw my life as a waste. To stop now? How could I stop now and acknowledge that thirty-seven years of counting, number by number, was a wasted, stupid task. My resolve to count on returned with the great peace of knowing my sister was now mistress of the house maintaining this sanctuary for me to continue my work. I sharpened my pencils more often. I formed each number with greater deliberation slowing me down but improving my accuracy immeasurably. I would never make that mistake again.

Another year passed. Then another. My count continued. Sometimes my goal seemed closer, other times farther away than ever. For some time I had had a doubt or two that the number even existed. Long ago I reached the boundary of the last known prime number and had, for so long, been wandering in the unknown. The numbers were of such magnitude that I often trembled at each new number and my mind staggered. They were of a size that was unimaginable. Determining the number of human hairs needed to form a path between here and the moon was nothing compared to my task; and what if those hairs were all blond?

Logic told me it must exist and only greater efforts would reap me my long awaited reward. But I had come to realize that this longed for number was only one stop on a journey into infinity, for after this prime number was revealed surely there must be another, and another, and yet another. There is no firm boundary, oh, one exists but in a different way than I first imagined. There are no walls creating separation, no valleys that divide, no mountains obstructing, no frontier at land's end. But I shall know it when I arrive it, my prime number, mine.

Through the gap in the curtains I have noticed how, with each passing day—as the count grows, the numbers increase—a unique light, an almost strange illumination that I have never seen before, not even in my faintest dream, enters the room, sweeps across my desk and covers the wall.

But there is bad news tonight as well. My sister, watching television, brings me word of a project from MIT. Students in a club there may be as close as I am to finding the next prime number. They have been playing around. The rumor is it amounts to a hundred thousand digits but they are aided by some super computing device which reduces the count of days to a few seconds. No. They will never count it before I. I have had forty years to count, forty years, day after day after day to count. I will beat them. I'm sure.

The curtains are open now. The tape has lost its adhesive quality from time or climate or evaporation of the sticking substance. I have allowed myself a few moments away from my desk to look outside. Of course there are changes in the neighborhood. The cars look sleek and unfamiliar and many of the people on the street are black. The trees have thinned though what foliage is there is quite green. My father's chair is beneath my window, rusted now and listing to the left. There are many more houses than I last remember. My sister didn't bring me breakfast and I wonder what is keeping her.

I have no regrets about the pursuit of my Grail. It is pure and holy work of the mind, honest and clean and necessary. I have no regrets of the joys I may have abandoned in what some might see as a foolish quest. No, for some time a strange longing has come to me at night, just before I settle down after the late hour counting session. The work goes more and more slowly as the numbers grow huge as to be unmanageable. But always, always, my curse—divisible by something. No, this longing is not regret for that which I gave up, that which I never had, it is an impatience to know the unknown lands toward which I am moving, to find the number, to claim it as my own.

The Three Bears:
A Retelling

WE NEVER SPENT MUCH TIME at the country house. A few weekends toward the end of the season when the leaves were at their highest color. Maybe if I'd had more time to prepare, if we went there more often. I can't say yet. Fifteen years of looking back on the events of that week. Fifteen years of introspection and therapy and rehabilitation, and I still can't state with certainty that it was us—or her.

What a failure of contemporary psycho-therapy. Sessions every week for a decade and a half and still I'm a bear. I see the world as a bear sees the world. I have my natural cycles. Some witness the primal event of parents coupling and are never the same. When she went out that door, nothing, not anything, would be the same for me, ever.

Was it us or her? The simplicity of such oppositions were evident to me when I was younger. The embraceability of the dialectic: A family in equilibrium is destroyed by the entrance of one young blond girl.

I assume you know the story, at least the way the popular press chooses to tell it. A vacationing family leaves their breakfast to cool and goes out for an appetite-encouraging walk among nature. Upon their return the famous lines: Someone's been sitting in my chair. Someone's been eating my porridge. Someone's been sleeping in my bed—and there she is. I've condensed the litany you've no doubt heard recently on the anniversary talk shows, on MSNBC. I was frightened to hear Larry King perform a dramatic reading of the tale. He should retire, the sycophant. The story *plays* well. Good and evil are clearly defined. The action is brief, taut, the resolution final. But is anything in life as direct, as univocal as it is in journalistic reports? You would be led to believe the entire episode was finished in a couple of minutes. But that does not describe the whole. We knew her. I knew her. Of course someone's been sleeping in my bed—and there she is. Where would you expect her to be? I had been sleeping with her for a year.

She had wanted to be a poet, I can't say why. Who among us would wish for that lonely pursuit. Every day you confront the blank page, perhaps scrawl a few words. For years the authorities have said the poets are crazy. They should be locked up. They are *special*, more sensitive, impractical, ridiculous.

A day's work is a good line and what is there to show for it? How has society benefited? How is anyone's life improved?

She once wrote: "My grandmother made all these pillows / my favorite now is this blue with gold trim / and tassels." They're lovely lines for their descriptive simplicity and the plaintive feeling they evoke. Meanwhile the persecution of minorities continues—my people included, we may yet destroy the Middle East, the educational standards of the country have slipped another notch, crime may be diminishing but its degree of savagery is on the rise.

She had a fragile talent that was never properly nurtured by any male she came in contact with. I say nothing about myself because by the time she came to me she wasn't writing. We had different issues between us, a bear and a human girl, inter-species intercourse. Oh much more than poetry was between us.

But I think it's important that you know about her. She took a degree in writing from a small mid-western college. School prepared her to understand the independent clause. Beyond that, she had little grammar. She went to New York.

Her move to New York strikes me as a bold, bold move for a woman who had never lived in a city with a population in excess of fifteen thousand. She found a rat hole in the East Village. A closet for a thousand a month with a hotplate, sink and bath-room open to the one room. She read the *Village Voice* and stood up at open reading nights at the Nuyorican, Cafe Mocha, Java Village, the Barnes & Noble near Columbia. She received polite applause and outrageous offers from bald men for group sex. Once she let one take her to The Cavern, her first exposure to S&M. Leather and bondage and fisting, she was shocked. Too shocked to put any of it in her poems.

She sent out her work and got back coffee-stained envelopes with form notes saying, No thank you not this time we have read your work with interest and chosen not to use it decided against it as it doesn't fit our needs at this moment good luck placing it elsewhere. Those were the notes of encouragement. Sometimes there was no rejection, no work, just her return envelope, empty. It became a great puzzle to try and figure out who—which pub-lication—had snubbed her.

She thought poetry mattered in a world where most people saw it on the level of roses are red, violets are blue, a thousand hacks on America Online "writing from the heart" who might better spend their time watching television, others watching re-runs of "The Tonight Show" where an increasingly infirm James Stewart wandered onto the set to read work that started: See that old wood rocking chair / sittin' over there.

She had a brief affair with a well-known older female poet who taught at the Newest New School, a woman who intro-duced her to the page-long caesura, to the book-length ellipsis. "Words are at a premium," the famous poet said. "You should never say the same thing twice." As "good bye" is simply an itera-tion of "hello" from a different direction, the famous poet stopped returning her calls.

The baby bear. As this I am remembered.

The one with the smallest chair.

A young bear sits on a chair. See that young bear sittin' over there. The she-bear thus accosted rends the peasant tooth and nail. For the female of the species is more deadly than the male. Like they have the lock on it.

I'm trying to find an outlet for my bearishness, and it's not in verse or in this writing. But this is the best I can do in a world which develops "bear–people conflict prevention plans" when confronted with bear management situations. The intent is to define appropriate courses of action to minimize the probability of bear–people conflicts while maintaining natural populations of grizzly and black bears throughout protected areas. Of course you can never trust a bear.

Be bear aware.

Make your house and garden bear-proof.

One of the most powerful attractants to bears are fish entrails, and all blacks have rhythm and Hispanics are lazy and Asians can't drive.

How about some bear facts? Grizzlies can run at speeds of thirty miles per hour. A collection of bears is called a sleuth. The largest bears weigh more than 800 pounds and can accelerate to maximum velocities in three steps. Bears are omnivorous mammals. No human, not many animals, can outrun one. You won't find a strictly vegan bear. Bears live for up to thirty years. I got 1700 on my SAT's. They possess a keen sense of smell. Here I introduce the Other as if I, too, lack such faculty.

Ursus maritimus
Ursus arctos
Ursus americanus
Selenarctos thibetanus
Helarctos malayanus
Melursus ursinus

Tremarctos ornatus
Ursus americanus
the family Ursidae
order Carnivora
Ursus arctos horribilis
Ursus arctos middendorfii

Most of the time, when I wasn't in school, I was by myself. That's the usual situation. If we were wild bears my parents would have taught me how to hunt and then sent me off to live my life, take a mate when necessary in the spring, hibernate. In most families, young bears, especially young males, are not tolerated by adult bears. Young bears are forced to search for new habitats.

We weren't your average bears.

We had made it out of the Arcadian ghetto and vaulted into the middle-class. My father was an eco-systems consultant, a job that kept him on the road most of the year. He hooked up with my mother in the spring but after her first litter consisting of me, she told the old man no more cubs. I don't think he minded. We sat around and ate a lot of fish and berries and plants. Lox is one of our favorites.

And I was alone otherwise.

Remember: If you spot a bear in a residential area or in a tree with people nearby, remain calm. Often, the bear is just passing through and, if it finds no food source, will simply move on. Keep away from the bear. Warn others to keep away as well, and bring your children and pets into the house. If the bear appears to be threatening, persistent, or aggressive, call the Conservation Officer in your area. If there is no Conservation Officer in your area, phone local police. If conflict should occur, do not attempt to resolve it yourself. The Conservation Officer is a professional and has been trained to deal with wildlife.

I didn't see another bear until I was five, on a school outing. The children taunted me when they saw a bear at the zoo. We were in no way related. He was black and I'm brown. That didn't stop the taunts. You've seen one bear you've seen them all. The kids could only tell the difference when size or color variation were pronounced. They couldn't possibly confuse me with a polar bear or with a panda or a koala.

Keep your camp odor free.

I was drawn to sad country music. If I had to run, if I had to crawl, if I had to bounce five or six red balls, I find a way to get to you. That's one of my favorites, that and drop-kick me Jesus through the goal-posts of life, end over end through them righteous uprights. She loved to hear me sing in my deep bass voice.

My father had warned me about being involved with human girls. "It's all right to be polite in public," he said. "We expect you to be polite. You have a family name to uphold, and a legacy. But you need to keep to your kind."

It may have been the right advice.

Whatever you may have heard about that morning is not true. It was our habit to take a walk while the porridge cooled but parents were not supposed to be at the country house that day. My father and mother had run down to New York for a business meeting and social dinner. They planned to stay the entire weekend, visit relatives who lived by the Bronx Zoo. A death in the family of their business associate cut things short, and they decided to salvage the weekend by coming out to the house.

What was I supposed to do that morning with her in my bed? They arrived when we were sleeping and I didn't know they were in the house until I came downstairs to make her a breakfast in bed. After that, events rolled out and I don't think I could have stopped them or changed things if I tried.

It wasn't that someone had sat in the chair or tried the porridge or slept in the other beds. That's not how they found out. They had brought me gifts from the city and followed me to my room. Over my protests of needing privacy, they followed behind.

"What are you hiding up there?" my father said truly believing he was teasing me. "Since when don't you want us in your room?"

Someone had been sleeping in my bed—and there she was. Golden hair askew. Her cheeks sanguine and full with the puffiness of sleep. Others might have seen her as red and swollen but for me she lay there with mouth slightly open, her face relaxed, still sleeping deeply.

My mother screamed. My father demanded to know what was happening. She woke up.

What could I tell them? I was in love? We were in love? I had ignored every one of their lifetime teachings. Could I tell them love would trump any or all of the forces allied against us?

She woke up and she knew what had happened. She waited for me to do something, to say something, to finally admit the truth.

She was naked when she got out of bed. Unlike the published reports, there was no dashing out the window without her clothes. No broken chairs. No shrieking on her part. No tears. She put on her pants and shirt. She collected her cosmetics from the bathroom. She picked up her overnight bag. Her dignity was astounding.

There was a moment when she looked at me and I thought I saw the start of understanding—of forgiveness, maybe. I wanted it to be forgiveness. Then she went down the stairs.

The press arrived a few hours later, tipped off by a neighbor, perhaps the groundskeeper called. I didn't care to find out. Newspaper reporters and television crews thronged the house, blocking the narrow lanes leading to our drive, trampling the bushes out front. My parents told their made-up story about an intruder in the house, about the chairs and the porridge and the bed. I went along, of course I went along.

But it was before she went down the stairs, out of sight, gone forever, that haunts me. She began waving her arms at all of us, standing as tall as she could, waving her arms. In *Bear Attacks: Their Causes and Avoidance,* Stephen Herrero recommends using a low and loud voice, and she muttered at us something unintelligible but nasty. Then she picked up a metal flower pot sitting on a small table at the top of the stairs and she came towards us beating on the pot, beating on the pot, beating on the pot.

My father said nothing, my mother neither. We had not seen a human response like this since we blundered into a campground when I was very young.

She threw the pot and it struck me on the snout.

"Go away bears," she said in her low and guttural voice. Then it was her that was gone.

Of All Possible Rigidity

TO ENTER THE STORE with a cart and a list on a Friday night is to signal that he is a single man of limited invention. To enter the store with a cart and no list suggests he is only cruising. To enter the store with no cart and a list reveals that his life is chaotic. To enter the store with only himself is an indication of spontaneity, an acknowledgment that anything can happen, a herald that he should be watched.

He swings past the aisle of fresh produce figuring the night's return. One hand tucks into a side pocket, he leads with his hips keeping loose knees; his steps roll. He hums in the tuneless whispers of children who remember every third word but not the song. He tests the air seeking the essential attraction, past the avocados tumbled to the floor. The peaches are in dire need of rotation but the grocery boys are engaged with the corn. There is an old man pressing bananas, searching for a clue to longevity in the bruised yellow skins. Farther up, a younger man with his tie askew balances lettuce trying to summon up the spirit of the vegetable inside. Is the answer in the pork chops? Has she chosen to stand among the fryers?

The dairy case is deserted, cardboard boxes extravagantly piled with whipping cream and fresh butter ready to be placed into waiting gaps on the shelves. The boxes sweat with condensation and moisture stains their fronts. The restocking is beginning.

Changing pockets, he walks past displays of gaudily-covered cookbooks and chilies ground to powder hanging in bags like ornaments on a wire tree. From what ovens does such food emerge? Certainly none he has ever known. Without pause his circuit brings him past the whole-beaned coffee redolent with steam, past the rice and the pasta and the twenty-six varieties of tomato sauce. One Friday he stood for twenty minutes talking to her-who-might-be-the-one. In the end she scorned his choice of low-fat dressing, left him standing alone on aisle three. She was nothing real.

Tonight he is alone on aisle three with the mustards, unaccompanied through the soups. She is not there in the bottled juices, in the baking section asking for help with the flour nor in the aisle whose shelves are filled with oil. It is only midnight on a Friday, perhaps too early to snare the returning crowd. Still he has had success on other Fridays in this store at this time wearing the same gray shirt and the same pair of pants, his hair cut the identical length. He has chosen it after careful attention to the new romantic comedies, and the ones released on tape which might entice her not to shop. He has reviewed the television section of the paper and considered whether a local concert might be too big a draw. There are no such distractions this evening and the store's deserted floor is hard to fathom. He considers changing tactics, altering the stalking ground. Where are you, my Angel?

He stops in front of the spices to reorient himself. Why does no one turn the labels face front? Order is important, without it, how can anyone read? There is the sound of rubber on the washed linoleum floor. A cart flashes by at the far side of the aisle, he thinks he catches the hint of long hair and an attractive posture. Only another musician buying snacks, long hair rustling in back, low-slung jeans. *Quelle* mistake.

He turns a corner and moves from shadow into outer darkness. He listens for the sound that might have gotten by him, only steady light.

He makes his way, childless, through the personal hygiene products, past the shelves stacked neatly with blue and red containers of toothpaste and fresh, gleaming brushes of all possible rigidity. He fingers the boxes feet numb with the weight of walk-ing.

This may be her, there at last, in front of the refrigerated cheeses, small and dark and wearing a man's white T-shirt, thin blue skirt bound at the waist. Her hair is shoulder-length and swinging as she bends down to take up a pack of shredded ched-dar. He grabs a gallon jug of bottled water and moves to her side, each step intention. He will ask her about dips and salsa, about Mexican cooking and do you live nearby.

He is next to her now and as if sensing him, she wheels around. A frown. Right hand against the cheek.

And the clear stone mocks the tilt of a chin.

I can't understand you, she says.

You shouldn't talk to me like that, she says.

I don't think so," she says,

He pays for his water at the 10-item or less checkout stand using small bills. She is two cashiers away, bent over and writing out a check for her frozen delicacies. Her skirt is slit on both sides and the shadow of her underwear is visible underneath. Nothing bold in this: her hint at revelation, feinting with bare skin uncovers nothing that tells—even the nipples are battened down beneath a white-lace bra, and the panties conventionally wide. Her body has a touch of hunching, suggesting a calcium deficient future.

And there is the ring.

She is not here tonight, will not be here tonight. He knows that now, tasting nothing of her smooth skin in the air—only her idea sensed within the shadows by the door. When he has at last walked the last display of fresh fish resting in ice beds laid out by married workers, filled a basket with five perfect nectarines, swept down the even aisles and carried off his goods to the line, stretched in the cool, waiting, found the bones of his back in their deep cracking, limbered out his knees, he may find her then. He has named her Ellen, glad and ready. His search requires patience, the tenacity of a saint. He is getting into his car when the full moon breaks through the cloud cover giving him enough light to find the keyhole, to start the engine on the first attempt, to turn around.

Connecting

YESTERDAY I did something silly. Don't say anything, Jeffrey. I did it because I thought it might bring me closer to him. Okay? I broke open a videocassette. Of one of his films. Took it all apart.

"Which one?"

—Which one? What do you mean which one?

"Which film, Elise?"

—One of them. Why does it matter?

"Your choice might be significant."

—What? It was…'Welcome To The Funhouse'. No. It was 'Welcome Back To The Funhouse'. I don't know which one it was. Stop interrupting. So I broke open the box and took out all the tape. Then I wrapped myself up like a mummy.

"Did it work?"

—Work?

"Did it bring you closer?"

—No. Something was wrong with the tape and it turned my skin all brown.

—Whirl is King. Work is catharsis. I find security in it. No one can find you if you don't know where you're going. But I intend to be found.

"Stan, it's…Jesus, it's two A.M."

—That's why I'm at peace when I'm in the middle of things. Working out story ideas. Pitching. That's what matters. You know Sartre said—

"Stan, this is Stan isn't it?"

—What does that mean?

"Didn't you just tell me last week how stressed out you are, how much you hate this business?"

—Last week was a bad week.

—I hate dating, Jeffrey. Oh why did Stan have to be like this. Why do things always turn out this way. You sleep with someone and then they don't want you.

—Bothered? By her? No, I'm not bothered. I'm not really thinking about it. I might miss the sex. For a while. But there's a lot of young girls out there that like older men. I'll meet someone else. Look, got to hop.

☙•❧

"Happy Memorial Day. I can't come to the phone right now, but if you're looking for Jeffrey Weinberg—of the New England Weinbergs—you've got the right number. Please leave your message at the beep."

—Hey, we're coming down, and we're not leaving. Ever. Pick up. Are you there? Pick up. All right, we'll look for you on the beach. You've got to meet the new lady.

—Hi, Jeffrey.

—That was her. Nice, huh? Keep the sand warm.

☙•❧

—Jeffrey? It's Stan.

"Yes, Stan."

—I didn't wake you? I had to talk. My house is so quiet, I can hear every little noise. I took a pill and the damn thing did nothing.

"Because of Elise?"

—Of course it's because of Elise. I've been thinking about her. I've been thinking about her in terms of us. You know there could have been an us—her and me. She could have been part of everything, my work, my life. I have to emphasize the word, *part*. But isn't part better than nothing?

—Do you know that brown won't wash off. I tried everything and I'm still yucky brown. My arms are raw from scrubbing. I may have to see a doctor. You know it's like no matter how much soap I use, I can't get him off me.

—But it's over now. Stan is alone again. Not completely, pard. You and I are going to make a little history, any day now. But it's over with Elise. She'll see that. I'm not keeping you up, am I?

—I've been crying for hours. I've got brown arms and red eyes. They're so red it hurts to blink. What's wrong with him? Things were going so well.

—She told me it was her that stopped seeing my friend Benny—that's how we met.

"You've told me this story."

—Oh right. Well I don't think it was that way at all. I think he dropped her. I should have known. Good sex doesn't mean anything. I mean she's lost all that weight and let's not turn the chicken—she's got those great tits. But…are you there?

"I'm here. I'm here."

∼•∼

"Hello…Hello…Hello. Leave me a message. At the beep. Hello…Hello…Hello. Goodbye."

—What kind of stupid…Hello? I didn't hear the beep. Did it bee—

"Hello…Hello…Hello. Leave me a message. At the beep. Hello…Hello…Hello. Goodbye."

—Hey. Your machine cut me off. I'll talk fast. Sorry about the police thing. Elise promises to keep her top on this time. You gotta love her. How 'bout if we—

"Hello...Hello...Hello. Leave me a message. At the beep. Hello...Hello...Hello. Goodbye."

—Will you get a new machine.

❦•❧

—Stan really rocked in bed. Oh, Jeffrey, I've never come with anyone like I do, I mean I did with Stan. I mean this was Great Sex, with a capital "G". Except one time when he smeared me with Knotts Berry Farm grape jelly and it had a bad reaction with my perfume.

—She doesn't have it.

"What? Doesn't have what?"

—That *je ne sais quoi*. She doesn't have it. It was impossible to talk to her. About anything that mattered.

"Did you ever say anything?"

—What am I supposed to say? Read this. Watch that. Do I look like Rex fucking Harrison? Get serious. Who has time.

—I'm getting older, Jeffrey. I want to date to mate.

—The more I think of it not even Rex fucking Harrison could have helped.

—I was on the phone with him for an hour and a half. It's always the same. He says he wants to see me so I see him and I tell myself I'm going to be strong and I'm going to cut this off. And then he looks at me with those blue eyes and I melt. I just melt. I start to get wet. I can feel it—

"You don't have to tell me this. You don't—"

—You could see it if you were looking down there. I'm sure he knew. And he comes at me and I just do whatever he wants.

And then I hate myself in the morning. I'm really sorry for calling this late but I can't sleep.

—There's young and there's young. My daughter's young. But I expect her to be young. She's only 18. Elise, she's 30 or almost. Maybe I'm expecting too much.

"Stan, did you want my notes on your new script?"

—Notes? What notes?

"On your script, Stan. I've got to be honest with you, I think it's a tough launch. I'm just not sure if the world is ready for a rap musical on the Rosenbergs but I have some ideas on Act Two that'll move it along.

—

"My notes, Stan. On 'QueefMaster Flash And The Bomb'. I've got them."

—I can't think about that, now. I'll get them tomorrow. Do you think I'm expecting too much? Shouldn't we be able to have a conversation about something else than these great shoes she saw on sale at Bullock's Wilshire? Shouldn't we?

ॐ•ॐ

"J-e-f-f-r-e-y. That is me. Who are you? Leave me a message so I'll know. Wait for the beep."

—Turn that down Elise. I can't hear his machine. I don't care if you're working on your tan. Turn it down. Did you hear that shit? Working on her tan. Kids. We're going to come down. Maybe in an hour if I can her to put some clothes on. Elise, turn that down. I don't even know if he got the message.

ॐ•ॐ

—I think I scared him. Do you think so?

"I don't know, Elise, I—"

—Yeah, that's it. I must have scared him. He's worried about his career and I don't want to work forever.

—She sounded like a tape loop when she got on the marriage thing. I'm focused now. Things could pop any day. I've got a lot of irons working. 'Scatman' is close. I've even got a shot to produce 'One More Time In The Funhouse'.

—I scared him.

—We were at my place, looking at the lights of the city. Yeah, it's one of the reasons I got the place. Chicks go wild.

"You still call them chicks?"

—What, am I showing my stripes? Or are you? Jeffrey, Jeffrey, Jeffrey. Chicks, babes, they go crazy for the lights. We're lying there drinking Korbel, naked, Astrud Gilberto is singing in the background. My faggot neighbors are quiet for once. I hate those guys.

—And it's like suddenly he's someplace else. Like I'm alone in the room.

—I had the most incredible idea for 'Scatman'. A whole new approach. Completely. It was a page one rewrite but I had to.

—He was stark naked in front of the computer.

—The ideas flowed. The characters said things I didn't even know they knew. I saw myself on stage at the Pavilion holding the Oscar, thanking my mother. I don't even like my mother.

—Typing stark naked. For two days. The poor computer kept beeping like he was killing it.

—It was the most important work of my life. I was writing the definitive comedy about the sexes. It was kind of like "Ordinary People" with jokes. She said that was when it all changed for her.

—If the script was the most important work of his life where did that leave me? And it wasn't even funny.

—I needed her to be there for me and she didn't think the thing was funny. People read it and roared, and cried, and were genuinely moved. And we're talking about people who have seen and done just about everything there is to see and do.

—It wasn't funny.

—Take the funeral scene where the body drops to the floor because the ex-wife is making it with the son behind the coffin— they roared.

—It was awful.

—How can I spend the rest of my life with someone who doesn't think my masterwork is funny? Can you answer that?

—I left. Came back. Banged around. Broke dishes. He didn't notice. Typing, laughing at his stupid, not funny jokes. I could have died and he'd have never seen.

—Just a little comfort. Is that asking too much?

"How'd the script end up?"

—It's in turnaround at Fox.

৯৽•৵

"This, is Jeffrey Weinberg, and I'm not available to take your call. I'm sorry. You may leave word or ring me back. It's up to you. I'm busy now. Searching for my narrative voice. Please wait for the beep."

—Jeffrey, this is Stan. Do yourself a favor, babe. Let it stay lost.

৯৽•৵

—Why are all men like this? Can you tell me? Why? They're such jerks.

"I'm not like that."

—You're not a man. I mean you're my friend. You don't count.

"Oh."

꼭•꼭

"You have reached 453-1919. I wish I was available to take your call, but unavoidably I'm unavailable. Or is it unavailably I'm avoidable. Who knows. Just leave me a message at the beep. I'll call you back."

—Hey, how's the search for your narrative voice going? Any luck? Hah, hah, hah.

—Don't tease him, Stan.

—Yeah, right. Listen, babe, I got these tickets for the bowl. Can't use 'em and Elise wants to go. So why don't you two go together.

"I'm here. I'm here."

—Screening, huh?

"What time?"

—You'll take me?

"What time?"

—6:30.

—This'll be fun, Jeffrey.

—Kids. Hey, have a good time, babe. You too, Elise. I'm kidding. I'm kidding.

—Jeffrey, we're awfully far back.

—Jeffrey, do you know anyone we're sitting with?

—Jeffrey, I don't eat meat.

—Jeffrey, I don't think I like this music.

—Thank you. Good night.

"But…"

"Stan, it's Jeffrey, call me back. It's Monday about noon."

"Hey, Stan, it's Jeffrey. I don't know if you got my last message. Did you? It's Friday night. Give me a ring."

"Stan. Hey Stan. You there? Pick up. Pick up if you're there. You must not be there. It's Jeffrey. I'm home. Wednesday."

"Happy Labor Day. This is Jeffrey Weinberg. I'm not available to take your call right now and, as you see, I have a new number. That's because I moved. If you leave me a message, I'll let you know where I moved to. Please wait for the beep."

Sometimes Rest Is Always Good

MRS. MIR-ABRISI WAS LATE. She hadn't paid either, though she promised the money and hinted at signing up for a full six-week course. The other "callbacks" hadn't and nothing else had booked for the rest of the week; none of this a good sign for the end of his first month at work.

Phil Warnecke paced the anteroom of the Max Astaire Danceteria. At the far end he performed a right turn-under to begin in the opposite direction. His was a natural flourish from years of mambo, hold, then two quick steps. The baseboards needed painting, the carpets down to the threads where thousands of feet clad in ballroom shoes had worn through. The walls, paneled with veined mirrors, bulged out at the bottom where the glue had relaxed from the heat of years of forced air. Yesterday's newspapers, or maybe the day before, were haphazardly folded on an end table, the edges already fraying from overfolding. Phil avoided all newspapers now. There was also a mix of old trade papers and a couple of *People Magazines* more than two years out of date. Who cared about Donnie Osmond's life in Utah? This was his first job after eight months of looking.

Down the hall came the clash of competing music: cha-cha's in Studio 1, lambada in Studio 2, some hip-hop tune in Studio 4 that Loquita, the black street dancer played for the Fogarts, a couple in their 50s trying to keep up. Studio 3 stayed silent, Phil's room, empty, waiting for Mrs. Mir-Abrisi.

He received a draw plus a percentage of every lesson he brought in. Mrs. Mir-Abrisi was the cousin of his dentist. Secretly Phil thought his dentist intended to marry off the widow, to anyone, even a dance instructor who seemed to have lost all other marketable skills along with his earning power and a house with a terrific monthly nut that had to be unloaded in a bottoming market at firesale prices. Temp work had been out of the question, Phil didn't type. Sometimes brusque on the phone, he despised taking orders. He had two specialties: he knew everything about land and everything about the mambo.

"We no rape," Saito, his nemesis had said in their final conversation eight long months ago repeating a quote attributed to Phil in a newspaper profile. Out of context. Hard to believe that one Japanese businessman could so have effectively, completely, thoroughly, bloodlessly ended his career but all development in Los Angeles appeared to have ceased as far as Phil Warnecke was concerned. The phrase offered a metaphor, no one was supposed to take it literally. Phil frozen out. A metaphor calculated to set the developers in the buccaneer tradition. Friends who used to fight to have him at their parties knew where their support came from. They couldn't help or didn't help or wouldn't. A bad joke, an unfortunate phrase; Phil gave liberally to women's causes—when he'd had the money. In their actions they revealed themselves as cowards, and in their words a sham optimism, always saying, Something should break any day now, Phil. We'll get back to you, Phil. Hang in there, Phil. Eventually, they refused his calls and left his messages unreturned.

Phil promenaded, managing three steps in each direction before running into a brown-edged potted palm one way, the reception desk the other.

"Jesus, Phil," Desiree, the receptionist said. "I just watered that plant. You know you have a lovely hesitation."

"She's not coming," said Phil.

"And the nicest cross-over."

"She's not."

"I did your chart today and Aries rising tells me you're golden."

"When are we getting some new music?"

"She'll be here," Desiree said.

"So you say."

"The charts never lie. But they don't tell me if now is a good time to buy. I found a little place they call 'Beverly Hills adjacent.' Perfect for me. Should I get it?"

"I'm not a man to be trusted," Phil said, "according to some people, so I wish you wouldn't ask me. I don't do that anymore."

Today was rumba day, not his favorite but who better than Xavier Cougat to take him through. The music intricate, the percussion designed to throw off the dancer, especially unwieldy Americans used to counting to four, but once a student learned to listen to the claves the steps came quickly. Through the thin studio walls Phil heard shouted instructions: step left shift, step right shift, now left, slow, shift, your other left, now reverse, step right shift, step left shift, left, slow, shift. That's it. That's it. Again. Step left shift…and on it went. He examined the albums available. The only copy of a record by Noro Morales had vanished, the pair of Cougat's worn and scratched, the vinyl warping.

He tucked in his shirt for the third time, trying to pull the front tight. It didn't work, his stomach pooched out, lately more and more he noticed, his pants snug. He could see the white of his pocket linings beginning to show, his suit-coat felt restricted under the arms.

In the studio he held onto the bar before the mirrors and flexed his legs. Because his pants might tear, he didn't try any deep knee bends or other limbering exercises. He had stretched some at home, it had to last the morning. Still waiting, he checked the shine on his shoes then the floor for any debris that might trip up Mrs. Mir-Abrisi.

When he warmed up as much as he thought he could, when he had checked and cleared the floor of anything loose, when he tucked in his shirt, again, for the fourth time, He put a record on. He placed a hand at his waist, palm pressed to his belly, the other outstretched and bent at a right angle to shoulder height. Then he glided along with the sounds of Tito Puento playing a mambo, his favorite. The music ran through him, gathering heat, streaming downward through his hips, through his legs, into his feet. The lighting changed, the music became louder, the conga drums pounded with his heart. He kept his back straight, his shoulders level, his head up. He glided, fluid with the music and its distinct hesitations, through the charge, the chase, an open cross-over break, coil turn, walk-around. A bulky man who scarcely seemed to touch the floor, he danced as if holding a woman, as if the music became a woman to whom he offered the fire of his movement. "¡*Ay Carumba!*" he shouted.

Applause from the door, and Mrs. Mir-Abrisi looked him up and down. Phil recognized the look and brought his hands together in front of his stomach. "Warming up," he said, squeezing his palms together, "and ready for you."

"I am ready for you too," Mrs. Mir-Abrisi said.

The abbreviated hour was not abbreviated enough. Mrs. Mir-Abrisi sweated easily, her perfume heavy and cloying. For simplicity, he kept her in a closed position using his chest lead, but she bumped into him, stepped on his feet, knocked him twice in the shins. She confused her left and her right, focused on the trumpets instead of the underlying beat. Whatever grace he possessed earlier vanished while he pushed and pulled her about the room as if she were newly sightless, and afraid. After the second kick, Phil stopped to see if the contact had been deliberate.

"Yes?" said Mrs. Mir-Abrisi.

Phil played a new record and returned to her side to give instruction. She placed an arm around his shoulders then dropped her hand to his waist and pulled him into her smashing her hips into his. Mrs. Mir-Abrisi had plenty of padding. He bent away and said, "That is not the correct position, Mrs. Mir-Abrisi."

"Don't resist me," she said.

There was a discreet knock on the door.

"Our time is up," Phil said, "have you decided on the rest of the series?"

Mrs. Mir-Abrisi collected her coat and purse from a chair in the corner. She shook herself and straightened her clothing. "You thrill me," she said. "You and your music, Mr. Dance Man."

"The series, Mrs. Mir-Abrisi? Have you decided?"

"Always the questions about money. Money, money, money. I think you see me as nothing but a paycheck."

Phil came to her side and took her hand where it lay in his palm, warm and moist and swollen. "Without your support," he said, "I won't be able to continue here. I'm sure you understand. The managers, they pressure me."

She seemed mollified and said, "Only if you can do better in your instruction. I may need private lessons. At home. I'm alone now, you know."

She held a check out, fanning the air slowly like a movement from the dance of the seven veils, waving her arm, her body swaying slightly. "You didn't think I'd desert you, my dance man?"

The blue paper moving languidly from side to side, one hand on her hip, the hip jutting upward and out, her weight forward on the other leg, her cleavage exposed, waving the paper.

"Don't move," he said. "Now that is the position. Feel it. Remember it."

"This?"

"We just have no more time. My next lesson," he said.

She brushed by and placed the check in his shirt pocket. "For today and two more," she said. "I may need many private lessons and I have many checks."

Mrs. Mir-Abrisi's perfume remained heavily on him and his clothing until much later when he took a shower and changed suits. Desiree happily took the check, "Didn't I tell you," she said. "Aries rising higher and higher." The manager was pleased.

"Way to go, honey boy," Loquita congratulated him when they walked out together. "They come. You'll see. Got to get out the word. Throw in a couple of spins and the fly-kick. You'll get them."

Phil celebrated with a large lunch and then dessert—pie à la mode with extra vanilla ice cream. He scraped the last bit of melted ice cream onto his spoon, combining it with a few crumbs from the crust and ate, trying to savor the last bite for as long as possible. Now too full to comfortably leave the table, his pants stretched and his stomach felt tight. Fly-kick indeed.

On the way out of the restaurant he caught his reflection in a full-length window. He was developing jowls. Except for the dancing, he hadn't worked out in months. His girlfriend had dumped him. His savings depleted. How many times did he awake wishing he'd never met Saito, never spoken to the building press reporter. All of this from one stupid interview.

Phil met Saito for the first time at the Riviera Country Club only a year before he was reduced to giving dance lessons to Mrs. Mir-Abrisi, only a year before when Phil stood on top of the world as top salesman of the month for Reese Management—six in a row. His girlfriend of that moment, the actress Tracey Smith, called him her top man. Top dog. Top 'O the morning. Top of the world.

Saito double-bogeyed the fifth only to send his white Titlist careening into a water hazard off a vicious hook. Some of the rest of the team snickered but Phil, taking a final bite of his nutrition bar, marched down the shallow bank and didn't stop as he hit the water. On that day in September a hot wind blowing off the desert picked up, ruffling the water. The grass around the hazard was trampled down but dry as if the water, only a few feet away, couldn't reach it. From somewhere a dog barked, and Saito's caddie began pointing and shouting in Japanese. *"Anno very ma,"* it sounded like. *"Anno very ma."*

Phil splashed in deeper and deeper, the sun glittered causing him to squint. The cold water shocked him but he didn't flinch or twitch or in any other way betray himself. He kept walking, each step harder and harder against the resistance of the water, and when the level was about waist high he bent over and plunged into the hazard like a pre-historic fisherman going after trout by hand. A few seconds later, he emerged, water coursing from his hair, his chest, his arms, but he held the Titlist covered by the brown muck of the bottom of the hazard.

Scattered applause came from the bank as Phil walked back out. He handed the ball to Saito saying only, "Two stroke penalty. Good luck."

The next morning Saito called and arranged an appointment. He came to the office flanked by two assistants, one of whom carried a gift-wrapped box, blue with a silver bow.

Saito spoke in halting English. It took five minutes for the bowing to stop. Another two or three for Phil to move the group past the secretarial area into Phil's office, the mass of people clinging to each other in lock-step, the assistants following Saito, Phil leading the way like some anxious shepherd. It took several minutes to choose seats, no one wanted to sit until Saito did and he, politely, waited for Phil.

Finally, they were settled. Saito spoke about the weather and how it was different there in Los Angeles than back in Osaka. A

different kind of breeze, a different smell to the air; it was different. Phil felt his gaze slipping past Saito to the Van Gough print
on the wall, the picture of the flowers, the original purchased by
a Japanese investor for millions of dollars. He willed himself to
continue looking at Saito's oval face and almond eyes. Saito
spoke about cloud patterns and how little it rained in Los Angeles. He enjoyed the rain because, after its cessation, it brought
out the most fragrant blossoms and he liked nothing better than
to pause from the busy activity of his frantic work day and consider the beauty and dignity of nature. He spoke about smog and
traffic congestion and how antithetical they were to nature.

"Many car," he said.

Phil nodded, saying mostly "yes," and "I know what you
mean." In the middle of a most difficult sentence on street lights,
Saito seemed to notice the gift-wrapped box for the first time. A
half an hour had passed. Phil's appointments waited, calls needed
returning, papers needed review. The day stacked up. His secretary came in three times but Phil gave her the look. Patience
mattered. Patience was crucial. Patience would lead him to an
unthinkable reward.

The gift was casually handed over and Phil accepted it with
a bow placing it prominently on his desk. He resisted the urge to
shake the box and guess its contents, to touch the bow, to rip the
paper, to open the gift and casually toss the wrapping aside. He
resisted the urge to even move the box to a place slightly more
out of the way.

More tea and coffee arrived. Saito spoke of a restaurant he
recently visited. Finally, he said, "Ah, Mister Warn-i-key. I interest in office. I buy. Yes."

"Would you care for more tea, Mr. Saito?" Phil said, standing to pour.

Nakamura Saito ranked as the fourth richest man in Japan. The fifteenth richest man in all of Asia. Phil discovered this the night before in the *Who's Who Of The Far East*. His volume had a typographical error rendering the title *Who Who Of The Far East*. The book dealer remarked that the error would probably make it a collector's item in a few years, worth some good money. Phil thanked him for that also. Phil had learned that Saito had a particular fondness for American food and American movies, a self-made man, a non-conformist in conformist society who demanded absolute conformity of his people.

Now, almost as an afterthought—the correct way of presenting a gift—Phil said, "I have something for you too, Mr. Saito."

From a lower draw of his desk he pulled out his own gift-wrapped package, black with white trim—traditional colors suggesting long life and health.

"Please, Mr. Saito," Phil said, handing over the package. Saito allowed himself a smile and a bow stiff yet elegant and graceful. When his head came back up the two men regarded each other.

"Tell me, Mr. Warn-i-key, you like scotch?"

෨ • ෬

Mrs. Mir-Abrisi had a neighbor who became a client, another divorcee but older and hesitant. Her interests stayed in waltzes only, safe music with regular rhythms she understood; Latin music terrified her making her hardly able to hold on to Phil's hand. She was no threat to Mrs. Mir-Abrisi who felt, he supposed, she could share her dance man with the less fortunate—and garner his greater good will at the same time.

An open house at the studio netted a few more clients, not the old nor lonely, but younger ones: a corporate lawyer who needed the exercise and possessed pleasant memories of long-ago cotillions; a hair-dresser preparing for her wedding who worried about the first dance with a new husband; a hope-filled actress, kept by a much older man, looking for diversion; and a young cartographer named Geoffrey who used his lessons to enchant women, surprising them with his grace. He especially wanted to concentrate on the paso doble. "My God, they love the throw-overs," he said. "They can't wait to get me home," giving Phil breathless descriptions every week. He seemed not to mind being taught by a man telling Phil, "I like the idea of one man passing on knowledge to another. My friends think I'm quite daring." Loquita gave up the Fogarts who expressed an interest in more traditional lessons and came over to Phil. Within a month, studio three became one of the busiest, and Phil had to buy new clothes.

His days began to pile up. He arrived at the studio every morning at about ten. His weight began to pile on as well. The more lessons he gave, the more he celebrated with lunch for one, big enough for two, then for three. One entrée was not enough, one dessert didn't fill him. He needed more. The *Maitre'd* recognized him now, calling him by name. Loquita poked his stomach and he didn't mind anymore when Mrs. Mir-Abrisi pulled him close. Though they were supposed to be in the open position, he let her. "Instruct me, my dance man," she said. "Take me to the stars. Only you can show me how." He bent her back into a deep, deep dip and she shouted, "*¡Ay Carumba!*"

The thin veneer paneling covering thin studio walls no longer depressed him. The scratchy records became familiar and welcome. He brought in a portable CD player and added to the collection. He knew the hard spots on the floor, the loose tiles. He steered his customers away. Every lesson Mrs. Mir-Abrisi pulled him close, and then she signed up for three more. She prepaid for seven months, full-time and the manager was ecstatic. "You are a real find, Phil-O," he said. "Where have you been hiding yourself. If I had you ten years ago during the disco thing we could have had franchises by now. *¡Ay Carum—*"

"Please," said Phil, "I hear you."

Desiree told him that his Aries had moved into ascendancy and lowered her eyes. Phil said he had to get back to planning the next lesson. Alone in the studio between those lessons, Phil danced to the mambo, only the mambo, the only dance that really mattered. He was a bull on the dance floor, powerful yet graceful, giving the music the power of his adoration. His feet slid, his hips swayed. His bulk topped 275 but he moved like a man with helium shoes, ball-bearing soles, the gift of a cat, the dance of water.

During a break between lessons one morning after nearly a year at the studio, Desiree showed him the real estate section. "Didn't you used to work for these guys?" she said.

"Put your money in the bank," Phil said. "It's safer."

"They're having some legal problems. I have a sensation of their auras being misaligned. Know anything about that?"

"They should have put their money in the bank too. What time are the Fogarts coming in?"

Phil excused himself to the bathroom. He locked the stall door and swabbed his suddenly sweating head with paper. He knew everything about their legal problems, their money problems—as one of the sources of their difficulties. They were coming after him. Any time now, firing an insufficient penalty.

Phil remembered the day, the day he meant to sign the papers with Saito, to close on one of the biggest projects and he and his company had ever undertaken. He was ready for it. He had worked toward it. He deserved it. He wore the suit, his deal suit, the closer. A charcoal gray, beautifully appointed garment, it had been hand-made by a tailor who died shortly after he finished the work. It may even have been the last suit he ever created. They were going to sign that day, Saito and his group, on a large scale development project. Phil felt terrific.

He came into the office snapping his fingers, moving between desks, he hummed "Ran Kan Kan." The office was busy yet with an unusual quiet. Secretaries kept their heads down, and typed. Around the full desks, Phil danced, he swayed, did a couple of tight turns. Thin and lithe then, he moved between tight places, pulled out an empty chair and swung it about, pushed it back in and entered his office. He tapped on the desk, tilted a chair back, flipped pens in the air, bumped the window with this hip. They were going to sign today.

His secretary stood at the door holding the newspaper. "Have you seen this yet?" she said.

"Get ready for a bonus," he told her. "Get ready for two bonuses and a dinner out with me."

"Phil, have you seen the paper?"

"Cha-cha Cha-cha Cha Cha. Cha-cha Cha-cha Cha Cha. Cha-cha Cha-cha Cha Cha."

"Phil."

CHANEL HAS AWESOME SALES SAYS LA DEVELOPER WARNECKE the headline read in bold type above the fold on the first page of the business section.

"Great picture, don't you think?" said Phil. "They got my good side."

Saito's call came an hour later. "We no rape. We no pillage," Saito said. "We no have deal."

Fifteen million in fees to the firm swept aside in a nine second phone call, Saito pulled out. The banks pulled out. The deal evaporated. Phil kept his door closed, refused all calls, tried to figure out how to salvage the situation.

What was so bad about the story? "What was so bad?" he asked a tank full of Brazilian fighting fish that occupied the far corner of his office. He had revealed some of the details of the deal with Saito, a complex series of financial arrangements that involved Japanese lease-backs, stock exchanges, and a build-for-tax incentive offered by the city. The *Times* reporter, Rona Vasher, said she understood. On the very same couch where he'd exchanged gifts with Saito she sat wearing a very short skirt. A tight black short skirt that rode up her slim hips. He came across as an assertive, self-starting man. She'd been flirting with him, trying to draw him out. He understood that now. She made no effort to stop the skirt from riding up higher and higher and that was when he recklessly made the comparison between pirates and development. We're all pirates, he said, plying the high seas of development, because it takes a pirate mentality to make it in the development business. Her knees began to drift apart, she wasn't wearing hose. Sometimes in a deal you get to rape and pillage, he said, or something to that effect. Farther apart. Her pen scrawled. No hose at all.

He spoke metaphorically, why couldn't Saito understand? The entire Japanese language was constructed on ideograms that meant something else. Phil had never actually raped or pillaged anyone. Phil's word was his bond. He tried to engineer every deal so that everyone came out happy, although in the best deals he came out the happiest. He never reneged. Never. "I never reneged," he said to the fish. "Never." He told the fish he never went back on a deal, could be trusted and counted on to maintain a core of honesty in a business with dishonesty more often the rule. But he expected rewards for his hard work. No hose, hanging on his every word. He never got her number nor saw her again though she did send him a laminated copy of the story. One of the male fish darted to the surface, its snout smashing into the last of a litter of babies. Something to hang in a place of honor. With quick snaps of its teeth and shakes of its head it tore the last two babies apart and ingested them—just like that. A flash of movement in the tank, fish scurrying to all corners as the male fed, hiding anywhere they thought they could be safe. Then the male swam away.

Phil was finishing a second piece of pie, savoring the crunch of the pecan, the jellied texture of the filling, cool and smooth against his tongue when his former girlfriend entered the restaurant. He dotted his lips with the crisp linen napkin holding it with round, bulging fingers, wiped crumbs from his shirt, settled his bulk more easily in the banquette which gave a bit underneath him. Violins swelled on the hidden speaker system. A waiter came past with something sizzling on a tray. The busboy refilled Phil's water glass. His former girlfriend paused at the far end of room, surveying, posing, preparing, then she began her walk toward him. Phil stared up at her and smiled, waiting for her to say hello; they had parted on difficult terms—she dumped him hard and quickly—but he still felt great fondness toward her, remembering the many good times. The *Maitre'd* seated her at the other end of the restaurant, her back to the room. Not even a glimmer of recognition. All those nights together, making love, my top man, she called him. "*¡Ay Carumba!*" she used to scream. Phil ordered another piece of pie.

☙ • ❧

The lessons were going well, his client base growing, a steady income beginning to come in, but not enough to do more than pay the most immediate bills. He had to keep a roof over his head, power, water, food. He didn't have the house but his other outstanding debts were massive, wracked up in his former life when he thought nothing about hiring a limousine for the entire night complete with a full bar of top-shelf liquor and a set of first-run videotapes, thought nothing of splurging on several of the best bottles of Krystal champagne, thought nothing of chartering a plane to fly up the coast with a full contingent of friends for whom he always paid, thought nothing of loading up his house with certified antique furniture and original paintings by the lesser masters and oriental rugs. All investments. Seed money. Priming the pump. An upfront outlay that earned him tens of thousands in commission because this made Phil friends, and from his friends came his deals. He put together Canadian tax-shelter condo packages over Easter brunches, new malls financed with locked funds while talking at the beach under the shade of an umbrella, shopping centers combining Hong Kong notes with oil profits while refilling glasses out on the verandah. Hail met and hearty Phil Warnecke, top dog, you loved to have him around.

He had to give up his house for a loss, lost his car to repossession, his leather furniture and his VCR, too. They took the big-screen TV and the home theater sound system muscling the components outside, rolled up the carpets and carried them away, stripped the walls of the paintings he had competed for at auction. Then a real estate agent relieved him of his keys, saying, "Sorry, Phil, the party's over."

Bankruptcy might have been the easy option but how low and dishonorable. Phil's bond was his word. He had incurred the debts. He would pay them off. Bankruptcy no option.

Thank God his refrigerator had been paid for, outright, that's all he was left with. Except for a cracked fruit drawer, it worked perfectly, resiliently staying cold in a world where he had almost nothing else though the catch pan tended to leak requiring frequent emptying. Though it took a substantial portion of his salary, he kept the unit filled with midnight snacks of Ghardelli's chocolate bars and four different kinds of cakes, not the fat-free kind either because he didn't like the taste. He needed butter in his cake, real butter, and plenty of sugar throughout, in the frosting, especially. No tricks to the taste buds, give him the real stuff. He heard about a recipe for frosting made with shortening and sugar, colored pink—his idea of heaven. He sought it out, found it at a bakery not far from work whose owners specialized in Southern-style cakes, and brought home two a week. On the top shelves, he kept generous portions of lemon meringue pie and apple pie and cherry pie and strawberry pie—when in season. He went through the list of all the pies available from The Pie House, trying each and settling on these. He stored packages of donuts in the door, and brownies way in the back. He had Snickers candy bars in the freezer along side cherry bon bons and Dove Bars and open quarts of Hagen Daas vanilla and coffee ice cream. He drank Classic Coca-Cola straight from the bottle, Mountain Dew, Dr. Pepper and Jolt, prizing the sugar and the caffeine which his body seemed to crave. For all the mountains of sweets he did discriminate: No jellied candies or chocolates filled with goo, no Twinkies or store-bought cupcakes or any kind of candy made especially for kids. His made one exception for the large jar of malted-milk balls that he dipped into while watching the news.

He had acquired a 13" portable color television, the tube going bad, a boom-box that Loquita sold him at cost, and a single director's chair, the bottom worn and stained by who knew what. He slept on his back on a gray futon set in the middle of the room, his girth raising the covers almost two feet above the floor. At first he rolled the futon up every morning, folded his covers, swept the floor in front, unrolled the futon at night. As his bulk grew he simply let the lumpy mat stay in the center of the floor, a sheet incautiously thrown over it, a rumpled comforter on top. Bending over to roll and unroll the mat took up too much energy; he stopped seeing his toes, and once down on the floor he didn't want to have to get up again until it was light.

The apartment had an address in the flats, the lesser part of Beverly Hills, in an older building with a Spanish motif subdivided beyond the legal limit. Phil managed the rent each month, on time, and the landlord left him alone. So Phil said nothing about the stained walls in the kitchen, the cracking plaster in the bathroom, the roaches under the sink, as long as the heat continued to work, the water to flow.

He had to get back in. He needed a project to concentrate on, a small property he decided. Something modest that his limited banking connections—still in place he believed—might finance. He began reading the newspaper selectively, concentrating only on the classifieds, perversely convincing himself that if he avoided the real estate articles he wouldn't stir up any of the painful muck that had settled around his heart. The property had to be close enough to walk to, and with his ever-looming bulk, the locus of walking distances diminished by the week. People moved out of the way when Phil came by, he took up the whole sidewalk. He had trouble squeezing through tables, he avoided aisles and began choosing the last seat on a row. Phil loathed public transportation, the other passengers crazy or homeless and the seats too small to support him. Without credit cards—taken in his fiscal collapse—he couldn't rent a car; he had only the choice of walking.

Fifteen blocks from his apartment, south, through a residential section of houses set so close to each other that neighbors could hear tea boiling next door, past a playground where no children played though the sandbox was carefully raked, past a deserted park where he had to hop out onto to the street to avoid sprinklers working even through the drought, under old growth trees trailing brown leafy streamers almost to the pavement, beyond the freeway teaming with cars at all hours of the day, there he found a corner gas station that had been closed for seventeen months, fenced with hurricane wire and boarded up. Vandals had managed to get on the property and spray-painted illegible gang logos that looked like Greek letters or symbols of the Zodiac. Trash had accumulated at the based of the fence, weeds coming up through cracks in the tar.

Perfect.

But Phil needed to gather some important data. He needed to know about the street traffic, its frequency and density during all times of the day, the business mix, how good the freeway access. What was the demographic composition of pedestrians in the area? Many questions. Phil posted himself on the sidewalk with a clip board and counted cars during the rush hours when could get away from the dance studio. He had started in just this way a few years back, young, eager, taking down the lists of office tenants in buildings around Los Angeles, surveying, gathering occupancy statistics, looking for potential clients.

Another mini-mall wouldn't do, the city was against it, citizens groups too rising up to stop unbridled and useless development. He needed a unique concept and a strategy in support.

He found the design in a German magazine on an outing to the library, elegant in its simplicity: An enclosed, multi-purpose space with underground parking. The interior formed an open courtyard around which customers walked or sat or dined. The exterior walls were windowed, the structure inviting the public to come inside. He made drawings, rough sketches and got an old friend who didn't depend on Saito's influence, to do the full-color renderings.

Phil worked up the numbers, put together a presentation. Still he ate. Still he danced. He went into another size suit, now a firm customers of Bray's Big and Tall Specialty Shops.

In his small room, Phil practiced his pitch, talking to the wall, preparing just as he had on every deal he ever put together. He worked on his timing, his emphasis, his hand movements. "Multi-level," he said. "Inviting the public inside." "Shadow studies." "Community participation." "Tenant access." "Local responsibility." Night after night he refined and refined and then he felt ready.

He secured an appointment with an independent bank in Beverly Hills, Middle Eastern money, another favor from the dentist. He took one more look at the site then, after canceling his morning dance lessons, went to the bank.

He was ushered into a nice-sized office, upstairs and in the back, plush carpet, a desk of dark wood, several conservative prints on the walls. A broad window looked down upon the bank floor through open slatted blinds.

"Nice view," said Phil, surprised to discover he had once known the loan manger, had minor dealings on a small project some years before.

"Mr. Phil," the loan manager said. "It has been too long. Too long. I hope you have not been having many parties without the inviting your old friend."

"No parties," said Phil, "I've been taking a sabbatical."

"Yes," said the loan manager. "Sometimes rest is always good, although not too much rest." He laughed and Phil laughed with him. Then he steepled his hands in front of him and said, "You have for me something? A jewel for my eyes alone?"

Phil handed over a folder set in a leather case which had cost him a half-a-week's pay. "A small project," he said. "Small-ish. Manageable. New building. Manageable tenancy. Something you could keep inside."

"Why share?" the loan manager said.

"If you don't need to."

"Unless there is a risk. Too much risk. We have to consider the risk."

"We will do everything to minimize the risk."

"Ah," the loan manager said. "And what have you been doing on your sabbatical?"

"This is a very manageable project, and manageable spells profit. For everyone."

"Our friend tells us that you have been teaching dancing? Dancing?"

Phil waved his hand. "Part of my resting."

"No, not you. It is part of your marketing strategy, I am sure. You are in the finding out. You cannot fool me about these things. But I am being rude. Would you care for coffee or tea or perhaps the soft drink?"

"I'm fine," said Phil. He leaned back in his chair and resisted the impulse to look at his watch. Mrs. Mir-Abrisi was his next appointment. He remained calm and focused on the man in the chair across the desk from him, stayed relaxed, acting as if this didn't mean his entire foreseeable future.

"I have never danced," the loan manager said. "I have not the nature rhythm. It made for the ruination in my first two marriages."

"Practice and proper instruction," Phil said.

"You think?" The loan manager had the proposal open in front of him but he ignored it. "I have a new girlfriend," he said. "Somewhat younger. More than somewhat. She enjoys, dancing."

"After we conclude our business you should invest some of your profits in a few lessons."

The loan manager swung his chair around to turn sideways to the desk. He leaned back and reached his hands to the ceiling. "In the home there was not time, we did not have the money. I am the first of a very large family. You, perhaps, did not know this. I had, responsibilities. So many responsibilities. There was hardly time for sleeping, and who could in a bed you must share with four other brothers.

"But I cannot blame my parents. The oldest son must shoulder his burden. This is how things are. It is why I went into banking so I would always be near the money."

He turned back to Phil and said, "But I am speaking too much."

These ruminations might auger for the good or the bad, the banker's face and posture gave no indication. And the loan committee had yet to decide. Still, the project could be killed right here if the banker said no.

Phil said, "I will oversee your instruction personally. It would be my pleasure."

"But why not right now?" the loan manager said, coming out of the chair suddenly, putting the folder onto his desk, coming around, opening his arms to include the room. "Yes, why not right now?"

"Here? We have no music."

"Surely you must know the songs. Come, we'll be moving the desk out of its way."

Phil stood with the loan manager in the middle of the carpet. He explained about the line of direction around the room, about leading and following, about starting from *the base*, and the loan manager seemed to grasp it all.

"That is all there is to it?" he said.

"Not unless you planned on entering international competition later this afternoon."

"Mr. Phil you are always with the joking."

Phil showed him the four positions of dancing and assumed the woman's role. He had to force the loan manager to lead.

"I am not sure," the loan manager said. "My rhythm."

"Listen to my count," Phil said. "Focus on the numbers. We'll start with the rumba."

Through the late morning and the lunch hour, Phil pushed and pulled the loan manager around his office, counting off the time, singing to him in a soft, baritone voice.

"Very good," Phil said, "Left. That's it. Right. You have plenty of rhythm, what do you mean? Again."

At the end of three hours the manager had to sit down, catch his breath, wipe his face with a handkerchief.

"I am old," the loan manager said.

"Nonsense," said Phil. "It's a lot at one time. There are hand positions we need to discuss, posture, attitude, but those things come later—after you feel more comfortable with the steps."

"This is exhilarating. Oh, the times I have missed. I feel particularly alive."

"Wait until you mambo."

"I cannot wait." The loan manager wiped his face again, then he took a checkbook from his drawer and filled out a slip using a gold pen from the set on his desk. "This is for the lesson," he said, when Phil tried to protest. "The banking regulations and all. We would not want for anyone to be thinking you might try your influence on me." After he handed over the check he said, "Mr. Phil, you know of course for the loan I must consult others."

"Of course."

"But I believe that my very strong recommendation will help things along."

"When you decide, if you bring the papers over to the studio we can work in another lesson. You should bring your new girlfriend too."

"No," the loan manager said. "I want this to be a surprise. I am so out of breath. Everything we'll be ready next week."

Phil was tempted to cancel all of the rest of his lessons but, until the papers were signed, until the deal closed, he couldn't afford any interruption in pay. Still Mrs. Mir-Abrisi seemed distant that afternoon. Maybe the dance lessons weren't turning out the way she hoped or they required more work than she might willingly expend or Phil hadn't yet asked her out or he didn't know what. She wore a brown, sack-like dress and seemed older, the corners of her mouth turned down. She didn't pull him into her once. The record skipped, Phil lost the beat and hesitated causing her to bang into him.

"You are so clumsy," she fumed. "What kind of dance instructor are you?"

"Allow me to show you the turn once again. Remember your hand position. It must be unique."

"No, no more coil turns, no more *Ran Kan Kan*, no more Perez Prado. Who dances this way? Shall we then pick the sugar cane? T-huh. I cannot stand another minute."

She walked from the room slamming the door behind her, rattling the glass, skipping the record again. Phil caught up to her at the water fountain.

"Mrs. Mir-Abrisi, would you like to take a little walk outside?"

This appeared to take her by surprise. "Why, a walk? No, I do not think so."

He took her by the arm, and her resistance melted. "A walk?" she said.

He led her down the stairs and into the bright sunlight. There were several other people on the sidewalk, cars drove by, the concrete clean as if recently swept. Only a paper or two swirled in the gutter. The small trees on the street were manicured. A doorman at an expensive clothing shop tipped his cap to the couple.

"Did you know I used to put together developments like that?" Phil pointed at a three-level retail group across the street, something fancier and more elegant than a traditional mall, a forty million dollar project with gold frames around the windows and new brick. The buildings projected upward at a step angle, the elevator stack, visible from the street, was constructed of exposed glass, the machinery rising above the levels and an interior courtyard.

"Suggested some of the design details. Anything to keep the client happy. Yes, that, and many more. You didn't know that."

"Just from your dancing," she told him. "You are so gentle and assured I thought it was your whole life. But I believe you would be good at whatever you did."

"I thought building things were what mattered, that and making money. I used to have a lot of money, did you know that?"

She patted his arm. "That doesn't matter to me," said Mrs. Mir-Abrisi. "I, too, have much money, more money than I can count. My husband..."

She dabbed at her eyes and they on walked for a while in silence. The cars passed them, one of the belching out a blue cloud of smoke which hung above the pavement spreading slowly.

"It's a lovely day," said Phil.

"Idiot," Mrs. Mir-Abrisi said.

"Pardon?"

"They should be arrested, such filth, taken away, whipped in public. That is how we would do it at home."

"Mrs. Mir-Abrisi," Phil said, "things break. Sometimes they can't be fixed."

"No," she said. "I cannot accept that. I will not. People must try harder. Even trees bend."

After the cloud of blue smoke dissipated a calm renewed on the street. No one hurried. Several Japanese tourists looked into windows. A limousine pulled away from the curb. An elderly woman walked a small dog, her manservant following behind with plastic bag and shovel.

"What is troubling you, Mrs. Mir-Abrisi? Tell me now. I am your friend."

"There is nothing wrong. Today I am in a bad spirit. It is nothing." She waved her hand. "I am thinking about home. America is so very different."

He stopped her and turned her toward him. He chucked her under the chin. Then he took her arm again and they continued walking.

"The aloneness," she said, at last. "I want and I feel and I lie awake and I have nothing. You cannot know what it is to be deserted, after so many years."

"Death is unpredictable."

"Death? Death? Is that what Morris told you? How he wishes to spare an old woman's feelings. It is the same as death. My husband found a much younger woman. They are somewhere." She waved a hand faintly in the direction of the west.

They walked on for a while until they reached a corner where Phil stopped them and turned to face her.

"I want to give you some advice, Mrs. Mir-Abrisi."

They stood on the corner, an unattractive middle-aged woman in brown, a young man gone fat but still the shimmer of handsome underneath.

"I do not want for advice. I do not want for anything. You should please stick to what you know."

"This is what I know. Concentrate on your coil turns, your style hand, the energy of your breaks. Practice them. Practice, practice, practice. Live the tango, walk with the beat of the mambo in your heart. No, no. Don't stop me. These are the things that matter. The music. The fire in your blood, the heat you feel, the charge of your partner and his chase. Perfect your moves and you will always find such partners. Never alone. I know this."

"I have felt that with you," Mrs. Mir-Abrisi said.

"Tomorrow, you will feel it again. Tomorrow, when you come for your lesson, wear loose clothing, something lighter, more festive. Put up your hair. Prepare to work. I promise you won't be alone."

After Mrs. Mir-Abrisi, Phil had only one more late lesson, and he stopped for ice cream on the way back. men rushed by on the street, others in cars talked on telephones, beeping their horns, careening through yellow lights, anything to get some-where. It took him a long time to eat. He saw women who looked like his old girlfriend, their faces carefully made-up, pos-turing and posing, but there was nothing underneath. He pushed his ice cream in swirling shapes, slicing the spoon down and through, bringing a bite to his mouth, returning his spoon to the dish, moving, always moving to the beat of music only he heard, dancing the mambo, executing perfect coil turns in the vanilla.

I Am For
My Nose Known

It does not, of course, refer to "carnival..."
—Mikhail Bakhtin, *Rabelais and His World*

CURSED NOSE, CURSED TALENT. On him the tempest fell that night, and he was wronged. Each breath of common air sickened him, the basement air, more putrid each time, the first stale wisps coming to him as he descended the linoleum-covered stairs, the scent traces growing in their intensity. As if the mountains had given back the scent of their beginnings every earth hole fetid with sulfur, he inhaled and felt a pressure. The burden pressed on his hands with a weight that forced him down, tired him, left him limp and dragging. His name was Hermann Zermacht Gorthundschweitzer and now engaged by a businessman for the keenness of his sense of smell.

He felt a tangible quality of wood breaking down—beyond dry-rot—into decomposition. The builder had used substandard materials apparent in the odor of their decay. With the next breath dust came to him, dust that lingered too long in the corners where lazy servants never swept assuming the Master never looked too closely down here.

And the next breath and the next: the travel of insects, fecal leavings of dust mites, dust upon scaling paint, water trapped under aging tile that never thoroughly dried, its bacteria growing with the muted rampancy of passing years like a gigantic bowel in stasis awaiting its first and only purge.

Smoke in the wood, smoke on the walls. Rank with the life of the cave dweller, the indigent piling up waste against the walls, the belly and bladder forcing its elimination down through the material bodily lower stratum.

Ancient fertilizer, bovine seepage in with the spring thaws or carried in with the fall rains, an admixture of like nature. Car exhaust penetrated even down this far, it bit a different part of the passages leading inside. Bituminous vapors wafted up from the sub-basement furnace that still burned coal. It caused him to snag each breath up short. He tried to open his mouth against the press of so many smells. Somewhere, what with all these clouds, and all this air, there must be a rare name, somewhere...

Gorthundschweitzer was aware of the hard stool beneath him, his old and angular pelvic bones pressing on the wood, aware of rungs too far for his legs to comfortably perch, his left foot left dangling. His nose overly long thrust into his line of vision. His eyes bulged to see beyond the nose. Over the top of his pants his belly rolled.

As he prepared, his mouth gaped open and his intestines rumbled with the crumbling of his last meal. Flesh and vegetable matter met the bacterial host of his gastrointestinal system, and the bilious pressure built up. In the close confines of the room whose exact dimension he had never measured, he was forced to spend a half-hour or so several nights a week, waiting. He had an inkling of the presence of the private entrance on the far wall through which the women came and went, talking about their dentists as if the business of teeth consumed them more than the business they had come to transact. He saw the dim light of the single 60 watt overhead bulb that glowed from a recess in the ceiling, heard a rush of wind through the poorly sealed casement windows bringing with it effluvium, known and to be learned. The wood panel swelled at the base of the wall from the change in temperature brought on by the seasons. He searched for earth, water, air, and fire, found blood, phlegm, choler, and black bile, accepted the belief that disease resulted from imbalance in the four bodily humors.

The cosmos surged within him yet the automatic nature of people who live in familiar rooms dulled everything without. A six foot pine might grow in the center of the room and Gorthundschweitzer would not think that odd or out of the ordinary or even something unnatural to the room. His eyes accepted. His hands accepted. His posture remained remote, until he breathed and the smell of the coniferous needles consumed him, this he would know before gaining his chair. The new aroma of pine, added to the mélange, would tell him something known but unfamiliar supplemented the room.

In a breath, he would know from where the tree originated, how long it had been out of the ground, whether it had traveled in an open-air truck or in a closed conveyance. He would know if it had been handled by lumbermen who smoked or drank or did not wash for days, trying to mask themselves with the cheapest of budget deodorants or hard-cut after-shaves. And as he would know this fictitious pine in every scented detail, the odors of the room came to him with a kind of painful sharpness that produced regret in each intake of breath. To pinch off the nostrils, for an hour not to smell. For the scent that never was, on sea or land. The exaltation. His dream.

Sitting upon his wooden perch, he never had to wait too long. Troames, the butler, his bearing grown supercilious with the task, led them in, slapping them lightly on the shoulders and back, the breasts and buttocks. They complained and he slapped them harder.

"You are paid for this," Troames said, guiding them down with a condescension reserved for his lessers. "Mr. Gorthundschweitzer requires 'musk,'" he said, his expression glorious in its reaction revealing how much the word pained him. The ritual must pain him too, his posture utterly stiff. He came from a great house in a manor outside of London, the son of the son of the son of the serving class, tracing his service back in generations of service. He never hesitated to announce this connection.

The Master had died without an heir leaving Troames, after the sale of the house, without employment nor a residence. A new Master beckoned, Troames followed—to America. Gorthundschweitzer had heard the story more than once. As his Master was exalted through business, benighted through wealth, so Troames rose up, out of the common social pit he had been introduced to in his new country. There was also, of course, the natural antipathy toward the German.

And after all, these were not even serving women: they were prostitutes. "Musk," he said again. "The slapping brings up the musk."

"*Yah*," said Gorthundschweitzer. The salt and the musk, essential for the process and for his ultimate decision.

Three of the women had been there before. Though his eyes weakened with age, Gorthundschweitzer's nose did not deceive him. He identified each of the returning women through a complex amalgamation of soaps, lotions, and other aromatic unguents with which they had anointed themselves. They had no cognition of the purity inherent in the simplicity of a single scent. If one was good, why not two? Why not three? Why not four, until the combinations of wood and wheat, vanilla, coffee, and copra, almond, apricot, cherry, nectarine, peach, and plum, apple, pear, quince, and strawberry, true roses, the most popular damask, and rue, evergreen and spiny-herbed of the genus *Ruta*, orange and satinwood, *Santalum album*, *Pterocarpus santalinus*, pepper and mustard, cloves and nutmeg and mace—and as if enough were not enough—broad suggestions of thyme and mint turned the beauty of each individual essence into a potent concoction known nowhere in nature, turned essence repulsive in its mix of chemical additives and stabilizers which mocked what beauty science attempted to replicate.

If the women had not been before selected, why would they be now selected? Unless they changed wholly in their habits—and they had not. From where did they come? And who brought them? So many questions Gorthundschweitzer had never before bothered to ask suddenly came to him that night.

Musk rising. Paid so much more than a night's work, the thrill of the dollars pulsed within them. They were not immune. The room's heat brought up their natural sweat. They were cautioned to relieve themselves before the inspection and some forgot. Cleanliness was next to Godliness and some forgot.

Troames strode up and down the line unaware of how much like a common drill master he resembled. With a blond mustache and the name Horrst, his manners were perfect for training new *Wermacht* recruits. The comparison would have horrified him. We stopped the Hun, Troames would have said. He stopped to look at each woman, continued his light slaps to force them into a straight line. Each one looked away except for Rosalyn at the end. The silence of clenched teeth loved deeper than any grave. Gorthundschweitzer remembered her name. She had brown breasts and the mouth of no other city. Rosalyn—she never looked away.

She said: "You hit me one more time Troamsie and I'm going to take out your balls."

He tried to slap her again and she parried his blow.

"You're in my personal zone, you know that?" she said.

"The musk," he said. "You have been here before."

The other four women laughed, the sound coming off the walls in renewable angles. The sun had burned her hair and it strewn about her shoulders wasted and long.

She said: "It costs money to step into my personal zone. Can you afford me? Do you want to afford me? I wonder about you."

Troames looked at each, sharply, until they stopped their laughter. Gorthundschweitzer was overcome by silence, the lack of wailing.

The other woman retreated into a ritual patting of their hair, into the smoothing of clothes not there, the shifting from one high-heeled foot to the other. They were cold, uncomfortable no doubt.

They were completely naked.

"It's just another dick, girls," Rosalyn said. "You've seen them before."

"The money, though, Rosey," one of the girls said.

"Ladies," said Troames. "This is Gorthundschweitzer."

"Is he the man?" another of the girls said.

"I am a man," Gorthundschweitzer said. His spoke in heavily accented English, his tones harsh and guttural. He knew Troames hated him, the Battle of Britain and all.

Rosalyn looked up and smiled. Gorthundschweitzer, in the weak light with his weak eyes sitting on a stool barefoot because he must be bare-foot in order to smell for reasons that he could never explain to any of his former employers—an Austrian brewery that specialized in a brand of particularly heavy lager, a perfume company in Paris nor his current Master—Gorthundschweitzer could not hold her glance. Here, the pliancy of box springs was not part of known equations.

Is the dwelling place of God anywhere but in the earth and sea, the air and sky, and virtue? He reminded himself that his job required less than a half-hour's work three nights a week. He had worked faithfully in the household for five years. Each year he was permitted two paid holidays—which he chose to spend on the shore near Fairfield because it least reminded him of his native Hamburg. He also had time off for Christmas, New Year's and Good Friday. Why seek other deities?

"Gorthundschweitzer," Troames said, "is here to make the selection. It's all been explained to you. Those of you not selected can dress and be on your way back to the city in a few moments, your tender in hand."

The process resembled a ritualistic inspection. Each woman lifted her arms above her head instructed, by Troames, to step forward. Gorthundschweitzer bent slightly, stiffly, inhaled on the right, inhaled on the left, then once more in the middle, the last deep, sucking the air full into his lungs. He was overwhelmed with the essence each time. His lungs rattled. His mouth gaped open, his tongue hanging, eyes bulging from their sockets as if the change in pressure pulled them from their sockets.

The women shied back frightened. Troames slapped them again. Gorthundschweitzer's legs and arms spasmed. His torso tensed. He sweated. He frame convulsed in the mime of the death-resurrection as the same body that tumbles into the grave rises again.

He brushed Rosalyn's breasts as he bent toward her, she had stepped in closer than the others. She shivered with the contact. Gorthundschweitzer coughed, lost his pacing, intent on making the correct selection, intent on a complex series of signals that helped him decide. All scent stopped for a second, no more, not long enough for Gorthundschweitzer to be truly sure. He was unaware of the movements of his body, the fear he engendered, unaware of the death rattle and the smoke from beyond. This, the first sign of the tempest, the darkening sky, the clouds scudding before the quickening breeze. Somewhere, there must be a rare name. He sat back dazed, wrinkling his nose, squeezing one eye closed, then the other, then back again, flexing the muscles of his face. Age was that adjective which began to modify confusion. The women looked at each other, at Troames, at

Gorthundschweitzer's strange expressions. The verb form was simplest in the present. He will go. He is going.

He is gone—and then they started laughing.

The Master had tried to explain what he looked for: "Clean," he said. "But natural. I don't like a lot of perfume."

Gorthundschweitzer coughed again and Rosalyn stepped back. "Again," he said. "*Bitte.*"

"We're ready for the next step," Troames said.

"The last one. Again."

Troames' mouth worked. He inclined toward Rosalyn who stepped in close again, but Gorthundschweitzer exercised greater caution this time. He sniffed quickly, one side then the other, and sat back, waiting.

Next Troames instructed them to step in, turn around, and bend over. Rosalyn stared straight forward, bent slowly from the waist, her feet planted more than shoulder width apart. Her buttocks flared. Her sex was clearly visible to Gorthundschweitzer. He was much too old. Barley was the choice malt of the brewer he had left behind. She stared straight ahead in the act of learning a substitute for love. Gorthundschweitzer traced back his name to the time it was first imagined, then given, then spoken aloud the sounds dissipating into a world. He spoke then, and nothing changed but the first voice which he uttered was crying, as all others do.

Gorthundschweitzer had asked the Master if natural included "the blood time."

"No. Absolutely not. How horrible," the Master said. He came to his feet, moved behind his chair, paced the high padded back between him and the desk which was already between him and Gorthundschweitzer. "Why the man making my initial selection should weed that out before they even get here. No, no, no. God, no."

Beyond the concept of "clean but natural," the Master grew inarticulate, and Gorthundschweitzer, used to beers and wines and perfumes, never married, reclusive, uncomfortable around most people let alone naked prostitutes, was unable to ask for more details.

Troames then instructed each of them to lift their leg and plant a foot, their right foot, in Gorthundschweitzer's lap. Legs did not interest him the way they may have interested other men. He inhaled once deeply, then sniffed rapidly four times on the last part of the inspection.

In spite of the dearth of specific detail, Gorthundschweitzer made good selections for his Master. He had received raises, and bonuses, all of which he banked steadily as if to wait some boundary in his life's remove. On the estate, Gorthundschweitzer had little use for money. His salary included all his meals and his room. With the purchase of a small stereo, and a growing store of special-order compact discs, Gorthundschweitzer wanted for nothing. But the year had collected beneath his face, he felt a turn down in the clarity of his eyes.

"Which one?" Troames said, "which one. This is taking far too long. The Master is waiting."

Gorthundschweitzer said nothing for a moment, staring at the butler. "Perhaps tonight you should like to make the selection, *Herr* Troames. Perhaps? You are in the hurry. Perhaps?"

"I only meant—"

"Perhaps we should let the women pick among themselves? What do you say? Since you believe this is nothing more difficult than the choice of a cigarette. Ah, this pack is red, a nice, delightful shade of red. The corners are square, perhaps I shall pick it. Oh, but no, this one, this blue, this is the blue I must have. What do you say, *Herr* Troames?"

Rosalyn was not selected and after the women left, as Gorthundschweitzer came stiffly off his stool, Troames descended the stairs. Tall, he had to duck to clear the ceiling.

"I only meant that the Master gave me instructions."

"Yes, yes, *Herr* Troames. I am very sorry. I am also very tired. This night was an unusually difficult one. The skill…" and at this Gorthundschweitzer waved his hand in the air, "the skill it is uncertain, not to be explained. I cannot explain it."

"I don't think you should argue with me in front of them. It is unseemly."

"Where the skill comes from, I do not know, and will it last? I have wondered this many times. I did not have the skill as a boy; it came to me."

"After the Master, I am the authority in this domicile and I must insist on your respecting my position. That is the nature of the great houses. You are from the continent."

Gorthundschweitzer looked up sharply. He sniffed the air sharply.

"What is it? What are you doing? How dare you smell me?"

"New soap, *Herr* Troames?" Gorthundschweitzer said.

Gorthundschweitzer lived in what had been a gamekeeper's cottage on the edge of the estate. Remodeling before his arrival restored the cottage to pristine condition. Wainscoting. Oiled wood. Each night the sky divided dark from what was known. In the heaviest gales of winter the small building stayed snug, a comfortable life.

He surrounded the cottage with flowers, blooms exploding with color at every corner passion fleet to the air. A root inserted into the ground by his door blossomed the next morning. Shrubs experienced astonishing growth, an inch or more a week reaching toward the sky above, the sublime beyond. Birds nested in the trees around the cottage filling the air with a barbarous dissonance of hatchlings following the mating cycle. The estate's feral cat population doubled, the animals copulating openly on the lawns.

In the still air of delightful studies, he filled his days with walks on the verdant grounds. Birds whistled in time to the mating cry of cats. Later, hours of lieder on an almost new stereo system and an abundance of decent food prepared in the Master's kitchen. *Ach* to hear Elly Ameling perform Schubert's "*Die Winterreise*" brought tears to his eyes and for a moment he stopped smelling. Perhaps it was not that at all. At the moment of rising tension in the piece, all of the odors of the world came together in the perfect, magnificent conflation without separation. Nothing foul was felt. In that bitter moment, there, sighs, lamentations and loud wailings resounded through the starless air, so that at first, after the tears had wet his eyes, he began to weep aloud; he began to rage in strange tongues, cursing his gift with words of guttural pain, in tones of anger his voice loud and hoarse, and with these the sound of hands, made a tumult which whirled through that air forever dark, as dust eddies in a whirlwind, as ash rises in the spiraling heat of the rampant fire. And then the change, as Ameling fell silent, spent by the effort of the lieder, Gorthundschweitzer's pain released as well, like the lark that soars in the air, first crying, then silent, content with the last sweetness that satiates it, such seemed to him that image, the imprint of the Eternal Pleasure.

The morning rode the whirlwind, directing the storm, the ocean sending gusts of dark-blowing west wind. Truckloads of flowers arrived to brighten the house, first bloom of the wilderness, star of the night. None proved satisfactory to the Master. Whole gardens uprooted for his display and none consoled, the blossoms trashed, scattering petals to bleed in the dirt. The driver of the delivery truck went around the corner and relieved himself on a colony of ants, drowning hundreds of them in his steady stream. Troames struck at him with a walking stick, driving the man back to his truck.

More deliveries brought pastries and meats and wines and vegetables and fruit, cellars emptied and not a happy cabbage among them. While the nearer waters rolled, the drivers pleased the Almighty's orders to perform and functionaries swept the steps, washed the driveway, raked the gravel walkways, cleared the lawns, pruned the trees closely while the tempest still high. On one side toil, hunger, nakedness, the drenching storm, desertion, and death; on the other ease and pleasure. The Master chose pain.

"How shall I be able to rule over others," he cried out to the sparkling corridors, to the waxed floors, to the polished wood. "How shall I be able to rule over others that have not full power and command of myself?" he cried as Gorthundschweitzer entered through the back, ready for his morning coffee.

In broad day the night again, all the activity surprised him, Maids scurrying through the great halls pretending to dust and redust books and cases and mantles and banisters that had already been dusted at least three times. Wisdom entered not into a malicious mind. The kitchen door banged open and closed with shouts and torrents down the halls.

"*Gott in himmel,*" Gorthundschweitzer said.

The cook's helper peeled an unusually large amount of carrots causing the cook to murmur to Troames over breakfast, "We'll be awash in carrot cake if the Master doesn't come to his senses."

Gorthundschweitzer was not overfond of carrot cake. It reminded him of his departed mother who used to force-feed him vegetables telling him in German, They're good for you, *Schnitzi*. Clean your plate.

"Perhaps we are to receive guests, a visit," Gorthund-schweitzer said, gesturing at all the activity. Then the Master would require none of his services for the duration of the visit. He that has patience may compass anything.

Troames pointed the blunt end of a carrot stub at Gorthundschweitzer who kept his features composed without conscience but the ruin of the soul. Gorthundschweitzer sipped coffee for which he had developed a taste since coming to the United States. The sun bled through the rear windows. He held the world in cupped fingers.

The cook and Troames looked away. Troames tossed the stub onto a pile of carrot stubs, a barrel filled with orange peel-ings, and soon, departed to attend to whatever butlers attend to in households of that size.

Within a half-hour, Gorthundschweitzer was summoned. The Master began low, spoke slowly taking fire, rising, became self-possessed stood in the storm. "Her feet, Gorthundschweitzer," he said, "her feet."

"Yes, *Herr* Bowles."

They were in a library filled with unread books. Gorthund-schweitzer had taken several down once and found the pages uncut. No words outside the scrim of his face.

"Well, it simply won't do. The nails were dirty and they reeked." The Master paced, his hand roamed, sometimes clenched fisted, at rest presenting a boundary beyond which the back wasn't shown. "Imagine, he said. "Imagine finding such a thing."

In the space occupied a moment ago—what has filled it now? Gorthundschweitzer said, "Reeked, sir? What manner of reek?"

"Bad cheese. Do you hear me, Gorthundschweitzer? Bad cheese. Must I spell it out for you? Coin is the sinew of war producing this." His hand swept the room, a presence in the knuckles unseen, fresh bones lurking beneath surfaces controlling movement. "Gorthundschweitzer, you are my staff. I depend upon you. Perhaps it is the money? The disease called lack of money? I can cure this."

"*Herr* Bowles, bad cheese. Blue cheese or Muenster?"

"Do you mock me, Gorthundschweitzer?" He stood by the wall, his silhouette reared up.

The German bowed stiffly. "*Nein, Herr* Bowles. I am for the particulars seeking. Should I know the specifics, it will not again happen."

A hawk crested by the window glass causing the Master to turn. The sun was hesitant that morning, smoke lay over the grass in a bitter pall yet no forest burned. "Feet are very important to me," the Master said. There was no space between trees, no depth to the sky, no way to escape shadows the thorn concealed. "Feet matter," the Master said. "I'm sure you understand my meaning. You are from the continent."

"I am sorry for your tension, sir."

He had not noticed the feet. He was not known for his sight, nor his hearing, nor his ability to feel. He had carried out the usual inspections and he had not noticed the feet. Impossible to know, impossible to understand, impossible to comprehend how he missed the feet if their malodor was as pronounced as the Master indicated.

There had been one other lapse in his long and illustrious career: an important batch of hops somehow fouled, millions of marks lost, Gorthundschweitzer initially blamed. Impossible to fathom the source of the skill. In another language flowers drawn against blue represents divinity. *Herr Direktor* had decided to have him fired. In French it was *fleur*; he knew many languages, snippets really, wine in Italian, thank you in Greek. There was an investigation by the minister of suspicion. All ironies were considered, and a resolution undertaken. The signs slid and a jealous rival confessed to poisoning the batch from spite. Gorthundschweitzer discovered the origin of words in their deferral, that granite made the better stone. He had not noticed the feet.

"Do better, Gorthundschweitzer, you must do better."

Better. Perhaps he could grow melons in winter and forget about wheat and if this were not possible, he might investigate the aridity of his nature, find ways to cool and if this were not possible, he would separate his fingers from the freight of his eyes and if this were not possible, leave the lights placid, feign sleep, and if this were not possible, he should speak softly and wet his tongue and if this were not possible, he might stand away from the door, offer no resistance and if this were not possible, to do better implied something within the man, changeable, something known. The storm came on and there was no containing it. Perhaps dust or pollen borne, a wind outside? Better, impossible to grasp. In his throat, the slight catching, his nose liquid. In the business world of the Master, to do better implied systems out of adjustment possessing a potential for realignment; it was a matter of calibration. Sneezes followed.

Gorthundschweitzer offered a prayer to the Christian God. What words to ask for smelling? Help me Lord so that I may choose women of sin in the service of my Master. Restore my urgent sense of smell beyond that of mortal men. God may be speaking. Help me Lord to root out the vile flesh with the nose and nostrils, gift of heaven. This, no trial but divine intervention. Help me Lord in the ministration of lust to divine the carnal with the protuberance of the face. Seen in a godly light what the Master did was wrong and immoral. The Master must be stopped, Gorthundschweitzer the instrument of cessation.

Scheis. Nothing but *scheis.*

Beer or perfume or women's bodies, he placed no value on the work simply the talent. Gorthundschweitzer walked about the grounds in an effort to shore up the linkages. In his attempt to identify trees he succeeded with pine only, his sense of it general, unlocalized. Desiring their first incarnation, he selected wild flowers from the woods and cultivated blossoms from the English garden, tested himself. He hyper-ventilated, straining to inhale. The birds of the air carried small voices. His neck muscles cramped and a terrible headache came on from the exertion with but an impression of scent plain to him, like hearing muffled by wool, like looking into night through dark glasses.

Better did not follow when he made his selection that night. He had to guess, looked for signs of cleanliness. Is not life more than meat, the body more than raiment? He examined the feet, between the toes. More light he demanded of Troames.

The master is waiting, Troames said.

More light.

Lieder did not relieve.

A visit to the doctor did not help. (Cholesterol slightly elevated, prostate a bit firm but no discernable masses. Blood pressure within reasonable parameters. The patient could stand to lose a few pounds which would help improve overall circulation. Reflexes normal. Sight diminished, as expected. Hearing diminished, as expected too. An MRI was suggested to check for the presence of tumors, something that might be impacting the olfactory nerve. In the absence of such a further investigation the diagnosis was brief: The senses go.)

More rest did not relieve.

Exercise did not relieve.

A change of diet did not relieve.

Facing Mecca twice a day did not relieve.

Self-flagellation did not relieve.

Hair-shirts and ashes did not relieve.

The Master was off for a day and so, with the burden of selection deferred, Gorthundschweitzer took a train into the city. The change in routine might help. The confusion of Manhattan's thousand charms might help, the vast array of available scents, a steady stream of correspondences. There were engines rumbling, wheels clacking, horns blowing, people shouting, blaring sirens. A change of lighting, a palpable excitement in the pedestrians as they bulled their way upstream. Streetlights changed and humanity pushed forward. A quickening of pace. A day flowing with birds, a ragged sun. Smoke hung about the streets.

Gorthundschweitzer made his way up the upper east side, choosing his steps. He walked past towering apartment buildings of stone and glass. All solace to man. Taxis buzzed the streets, drivers flinging their boots about the pedals. Steam geysered from vents. Past store windows laden with merchandise. Past liveried doormen in black with golden epaulets. Green gloss appeared on the twice-burned melicgrasses growing in the cut of the median. Past galleries of burlap and painted terra-cotta. Past oil and wood, his breath came forcefully with the exertion of walking. Past portraits of dogs in drippy, expressionistic brushwork. Of freedom and of life he was not deserving. Past a group casting in bronze. Past Tuscan landscapes and dresses of crêpe. Past Smokey Joe's, Alison on 80th, Pinang and Matsuhisa's.

No great scent came.

At noon, tired and hungry, he entered what he thought was a coffee shop, selecting a counter seat. The walls, covered with paintings, had figures coupling in all the Kama Sutra forms.

"Interested?" a waitress said.

Statues in alcoves of devil men in priapus. Phalluses hung from the ceiling, the rear door in the shape of an "o." An espresso machine frothed, its steam rising before the valve closed.

Too tired to leave, Gorthundschweitzer nodded when the waitress returned with a steaming pot and poured into oversize cups. Gorthundschweitzer circled the bowl with his hands and inhaled—coffee, it seemed, but in the oblique.

Then he was ravenous, his appetite for food gargantuan. With the figures of copulation about him he ordered steak and eggs. Chops. Two omelets with different cheese. Pancakes. Waffles. His jaws opened and shut. Toast and muffins and cake. Position 71 has the knees raised, the back curled inward. Banana bread. A club sandwich. Mastication, molars grinding. Chicken-fried steak. Mashed potatoes into his gaping mouth. Vegetables *au gratin*. Position 112 places the women on top, the couple breathing in unison. Biscuits in gravy. But no blood sausage. No blood sausage. Cake and apple pie and ice cream and lemon meringue. His gullet unsatiated. Pecan pie heated with whipped cream.

A cricket began to sing. A cricket in the city carried overhead. The cricket called, rubbing his wings unfolded by the wall, his rough cadence. The cricket wound his way upward, wound the long wind of his way upward in the noise of his beetle-dark song Gorthundschweitzer heard the wreck of the morning.

And Rosalyn walked in the door.

The whore from the storm night. She dressed in a light jacket, chanted foreign words, called out to nature, her hair braided into plaits like scarves of lilacs. He was not insensible then to the living.

She was about to walk by and Gorthundschweitzer excused himself, tipped his chin down to greet her. "*Fraulein*," he said. "*Eine* surprise."

Position 212 has the couple on their backs, legs opened, bodies turned one to receive the other.

"Are you out looking for them?" She laughed and said, "You won't find anyone in here."

Position 400 places the female with her legs closed, the man with his legs open.

"Would you care to with me eat?" he said.

Position 600 has the couple connected by only the tip of the genitalia. The couples breathe alternatively into one another's mouth.

She sat beside him. Ordered. Drank juice. In the beginning, she said, she was young. In the beginning she was devoted. In the beginning she was no different from moss grown at the edge of a rock returning after each disaster to start life again.

"And I am for my nose known."

"That's something," she said. "A talent."

And they spoke or rather she spoke and he listened, this much younger woman spoke as if she had known him for as long as he had known himself. Afterward he tried to understand what they had spoken of. His attention was distracted and what she gave, she gave with such ease that the giving stilled all questioning. She told him unnatural vices are fathered by heroism, virtues forced upon them by impudent crimes. Someone wrote that, he said. Yes, she said, someone wrote that.

Then she asked: "Are you busy for the rest of afternoon? Interested? I'm available."

"I am too old," he said.

"No one," she said, "is too old."

One night later, the basement ritual repeated. The room darkened. The walls grew closer. The women stood before him, naked, sweating, anxious; Gorthundschweitzer inhaled. He sat on the stool, his feet bare. He wore a three-piece suit, his belly protruding. He inhaled, deep to the point where forces shifted inside him, physical catchings, pain about his heart, pulling harder and harder, his nostrils closed by the suction, his throat scraped raw, ears popping.

He died, an old man on a dry night, perhaps not wholly dead but on his way to death, his lands disordered, head of stone and straw—then exhaled. Spiders suspended all operations. The world swayed dull in windy places. Red brick and no water and yet sweat coursed down his sides. Into his aching head sensation returned in the simple act of breathing, in with control, out and giving. The presence that so disturbed him, a sense sublime of something far more deeply interfused, vanished at once. The scent was absent, the air unbroken. Complete and total absence of scent.

"What is it Gorthundschweitzer?" Troames demanded. "Is there a problem?"

Gorthundschweitzer breathed in again, breathed out, breathed in. Metaphors escaped him. No chanting. In the empty room all shadows held.

"Gorthundschweitzer, the women are here. The Master is waiting. Gorthundschweitzer. Gorthundschweitzer. Gorthund-schweitzer."

"It is not my hearing, *Herr* Troames that is at fault. You need not shout at me. Bring them closer."

As before, the women came closer and were instructed. The slapping may have aroused a musk. Gorthundschweitzer sat impervious. For the first time he looked. Glorious bodies musculature apparent, angle of bones, breasts and buttocks, the turn of a knee, the splayed feet with toes spread—and the anxious faces.

"You are wasting time, Gorthundschweitzer," said Troames.

Gorthundschweitzer smiled, felt his mouth pull into the full vent of a smile, his mouth wide, aging teeth glistening. He was free, his body releasing him from the scent prison. Glorious to not smell, to breathe in and no—nothing.

And what now? Other men saw history, its many cunning passages, contrived corridors and issues, and were deceived with whispering ambitions, guided by vanities. Gorthundschweitzer had used his talent as a means to work. Common labor he had avoided and his intellect he exercised in the appreciation of his lieder. And what now? An old man at the end of a dry year, seventy dry years.

Rosalyn told him no one was too old but he had declined that afternoon, left her in the restaurant and returned to the estate. And what now? After this knowledge what forgiveness? What mercy?

"Gorthundschweitzer," Troames said again.

He was old, an old man, family gone, alone, no sons to follow him. Had he ever had any friends? A cloistered life as a secular monk suddenly freed from the tyranny of sense. He had said the same things to Rosalyn and again she told him, no one is too old.

"Leave us, *Herr* Troames," Gorthundschweitzer said. "I shall call you when we are ready. That is how it shall be tonight."

No protests were accepted; Troames withdrew. After that, Gorthundschweitzer got down off the stool. "*Frauleins*," he said. "One of you is to be for the Master selected." He took off his wool suitcoat, his vest, and folded them, placing them on top of the seat. Tenant in a dry room, his loss had freed him and now, though the strain must kill him, he would find another freedom. One last time. He took off his shirt, and with effort, his trousers, standing there barefoot in white boxer shorts. The floor was cold. Smooth. Solid. "It is a simple test," he said, removing his shorts and standing before them completely naked as they stood before him naked, too.

In The Space
Between Stairs

STAN WAS GOING to become the youngest stuntman ever. Not as an act of rebellion or accommodation because his father was in the Business and his mother had once acted, not because he craved speed or heights or danger.

"It's a great movie hook, very high concept," his friend Bradley said. "I can sell it."

They were ten. They lived a few blocks from each other, had been born a few days apart. Stan's father produced (hoped to produce again, had his name attached to eight projects that hadn't gotten made "Yet, but we're very close"), Bradley's father was an accountant for Larry Storch and the estate of Zero Mostel.

"Let's start with a gag. A big gag," said Stan.

"I'll get it on tape. Like a calling card."

"Something to build on."

"Yes," said Bradley. "The filmmaker speaks."

Stan was going to become the youngest stuntman ever, not because his father spent less and less time with him and tried to make up by buying "things" (then stood around with the other parents after karate class implying how much he had paid), nor because his father cancelled out on their last four scheduled "special times." Not because his mother had found a new career, cooked almost not at all, rushed Stan from piano lessons to tutoring in a station wagon with the magnetic signs of her real estate office on its doors. Not because his parents promised him a birthday party but the details seemed to grow more vague with each passing day—it was an argument over a satellite dish.

"It'll raise the value of the property," Stan's father said. Stan's nuclear family sat in different locations in the combination kitchen/family room/breakfast nook, a room created by the removal of three outside walls and the creation of a new space over what had once been yard, another project in the interest of raising property values. Stan stood by the ovens, his father at the round table along with the far wall with the bay windows and his mother leaned against the sink.

"Don't tell me that doesn't matter to you," his father said "I understand what matters to people. It's my business to understand what matters."

"They look horrible." She ran the water. She stopped the water.

"I need this for my work, my career, our lives together."

Can't you wait for those DB whatever?" his mother said. "The little ones?" She ran the water again. She turned on the disposal.

"What do you think, Stan?" his father asked over the rushing water and the grinding. His parents, children of the 60s, believed everyone should be involved in family decisions.

"He watches way too much television as it is," his mother said punctuating her words with the silence of the machines.

"He has to know about the Business if he's going into the Business."

"He's not going into the Business. He's going to do something sane. Something that matters."

"So what I do doesn't matter?"

"What have you done?"

And so it went, the argument one of many arguments in which Stan's opinion was elicited but not heard, in which his presence as audience was encouraged but his role relegated to silent auditor. Without Stan's answer and without further consultation though with several more arguments between his parents over the next several weeks in which he stood by (looking for an opening to discuss the birthday party, realizing the timing wrong, the timing might always be wrong) while water and electricity were wasted, fresh paper products hurled into the trash, food left uneaten, newspapers unread, mail not opened—arguments about money (his father couldn't find a development deal anywhere and they were forced to cash in the IRAs [at penalty] in order to maintain their lifestyle. "Thank God, Stan doesn't go to private school," his mother said. "He'd have to drop out." "He may have to stop all those lessons anyway," his father said. "He needs them," his mother said. "Stan what do you think?"), arguments about property values (Stan's real estate selling mother had numbers always on her mind), aesthetics (his mother favored classical Italian, his father—in an effort to stay in touch with "the youth" [something he perceived as a kind of beast, a herd grazing just over the next rise] wore his hair long and badly cut, sported over-size jeans and Doc Martens—favored MTV), work ethic, necessity for work—and money—the satellite went in. A three-meter gray, wire mesh-backed dish from Pencost Systems, with a Krugel tuning fork array.

"Details matter, Stan," his father said, pointing out the gold coaxial wiring ("Gold is better than silver [and 14 times more expensive]. Remember that."), the Stromson servo-control motor system ("Best on the market [if one were to believe the salesman who might be getting a kickback from the manufacturer for pushing their brand]. Best is better."), the Lymeton solar panel power backup ("Just in case, Stan [just in case the power fails and the family might be without a vital communications link with the outside world for more than a nanosecond]. It pays to be prepared.").

Afternoons after school, Stan had access to 147 different stations in 8 different languages. His father didn't block the adult channels though Stan was not much interested in the pneumatic blondes bouncing up and down moaning, Oh, God, oh, baby. (Didn't those breasts hurt? The weight. They must have strong backs and how did they sleep?) From sex education class he understood how the human species procreated, what parts fit. He was aware of the many uses of the penis. He had one. What absorbed him was Buck Simms.

Buck Simms was one of the first wave of Hollywood stuntmen. Buck Simms sometimes doubled for Tom Mix in many of his westerns. The popular press believed Mix did his own stunts but it wasn't completely true so Stan discovered watching a special on the American Western Classics movie channel. (Another myth exploded.) Buck Simms also doubled for Stuart Granger, John Wayne, and Tyrone Power. Too tall to stand-in for Alan Ladd and Audie Murphy wouldn't have him, there was plenty of other work. And who could forget his wonderful terrifying performance in "Fort Apache" where he played Indians in the night scenes, soldiers by day or *The Perils of Nyiko*, one of the most wild serials ever made where Buck doubled for nearly everyone in the cast, the heroine included.

Buck joined a long line of stuntmen that went back to the days of Sennet's Keystone Cops. Harris Gordon, John Lehnberg, Eagle Eye, John Epper, Richard Talmadge, Dave Sharpe, Joe Bonomo, Charles Hutchinson, Eddie Polo. Yakima Canutt may have won the Academy Award but Buck originated many of the stunts Canutt later made famous. Buck was a natural horseman and his horse work surpassed the best stuntmen because of his agility and his affinity for the animals. He did things cowboys couldn't do: a jump from a balcony to a horse, leaps between galloping stallions. He could work 10 storeys in the air because height didn't affect him. He was an athlete and a tumbler, and had the terrific timing and coordination not found in cowboys.

The contemporary stuntmen had nothing on Buck, Dar Robinson in particular. What did a bunch of high-tech parachute stunts add up to? The movies were forgettable, the stunts added little. Besides, Dar died in the desert, impaled on a cactus, without medical help. It was tragic. It was stupid. He fell off a motor-cycle on a practice run. The crew stood around for two hours and watched him die, the life leaching out of him. Not Buck though. Buck just disappeared. It was rumored he was seen going into a fire during his last stunt on a remake of "Remember the Alamo." The gag produced fine footage, a nomination from the Association, but that was the last of him. Who really knew?

To see Buck Simms leap onto a horse at full gallop, turn around in the saddle and fire both six-shooters, turn back and ride off into the chaparral, to see him jump from a speeding train, hurl himself through windows, leap from the top of a wa-ter tower, fall, as if dead, from the steeply pitched roof of a general store, take on ten men in a barroom brawl, drag behind a runaway horse, his leg "caught" in the stirrup, crash to the ground as his horse took a violent but controlled fall from a Running-W, drive a wagon off a high cliff, leap from the top of a dam as it exploded, wade in to herd off a stampede of maddened steers, rope and bull-dog with barely a scratch—now that's enter-tainment.

Not trying to sell homes in the Valley nor sitting in an office near (but not on) a studio lot taking endless, futile meetings. Buck Simms, stuntman, was a man of the outdoors, a man of action and bravery, a man who took calculated risks and made them look easy. He was a model for the future—Stan's future.

On the Saturday after Stan saw the show on Buck Simms and made his important decision, he was finally able to break free of his heavy schedule of the piano lessons, karate lessons, plus rotational tutoring in all his subjects. He did not need re-medial work, but his parents insisted on the tutoring in order to give him the same advantages private school students had. (Yet they paid as much for the extra lessons and tutoring as they would have spent to send him to private school.)

And they constantly argued about money.

He knew that his going to public school had something to do with those marches his parents had been in when they were in college but the connection was never fully explained to him any more than the word "egalitarian." (One did not have to be a genius to understand there was little equality in the world.)

On that Saturday Stan was finally able to get to the library. Though he was slotted for piano practicing, he convinced his mother that a book report due on Monday required immediate library research.

"You'll have to stay up later to finish your practicing," his mother said. "I won't be here to monitor you, I'm leaving for my open house."

"I'll do it," Stan said. His library card was in his pocket. He had memorized the correct spelling of Buck Simms' name.

"And why did you wait so long? When was this assigned?" His mother was weighted down with a briefcase and a collection of information kits on the house for sale. "You know you have to tell me these things. I'm not a mind reader, unlike what your father thinks. Scheduling matters."

"I forgot," Stan said. "I'll practice when I get home."

"And don't let your father try to get you to watch another show with him. That god damn dish. Until you practice. Then you need to run through your *kata* and I'm sure you have homework from tutoring. Don't you have homework from tutoring?"

Stan rode his bike to one of the last remaining open local branches of the Los Angeles public library system. Though the shelves were in disarray and the branch woefully understaffed, a couple of hours of systematic searching turned up not one but two books about stuntmen. The first was a history, the second purported to be a training manual of sorts for beginners.

Stunt work is an illusion, the history book said. From the most simple punch to an elaborately choreographed stampede, from an easy walk down the top of a speeding train to a full-scale assault on the Alamo, the stuntman simulates death in a thousand ways. With each new stunt, the stuntman looks in the heart of darkness where being and nothingness collide.

"Wow," said Stan. He hadn't realized that stunt work might be a calling.

"I didn't know that either," said Bradley. "It is a calling."

An effective punch grazes but does not connect, uses the lens' depth of field in the simulation; it's the sound effects that carry over. A stampede employs mechanical cows, close-ups of hide-covered wooden heads, multiple exposures from slightly altered angles, and again, sound is critical to complete the show. A speeding train is created by undercranking the camera. The simulated assault on the Alamo takes days to produce two minutes of finished film.

The book on training was perhaps more practical. He had to be in shape, the book said. He had to have strength and endurance but he needed to be limber and flexible, too. Stunt work demanded many different and difficult qualities in a person. Balance mattered. Timing. Depth perception. Physio-kinetic awareness. Stan had to look up the last one and was unable to discover its meaning until one of the gym teachers, during a lesson on the parallel bars, mentioned that the best gymnasts had Physio-kinetic awareness.

"Stuntmen, too," Stan said.

"We read that," said Bradley.

The class tittered. "If you say so, men," the gym teacher said. "Now, who's first?"

Bradley stood by with a notepad jotting down ideas as Stan began his training in the afternoons after school while his mother was off in the Valley selling homes. He'd been to one of her open houses. She stood for hours in the living room of the house waiting for the buyers. The houses she showed were always somewhat dilapidated. Over-priced. The yards untended. Like their house.

Five years before such houses would have been snapped up as fixer-uppers. "Starters," her mother called them. The market went bad as Stan's mother went into real estate. The boom over, everyone struggled to move properties. The houses Stan's mother sold had trouble staying in escrow.

"It's the broker's curse," she said.

She stood in the living room of houses waiting for buyers and she never sat down.

"Because it makes a bad impression," she told Stan.

"What about me?" Stan said. "Do brokers usually bring along their children? Will I make a bad impression?"

His mother squeezed him on the shoulder and said, "If anyone asks, you're a broker in training."

(His mother was perhaps more optimistic than practical. But she worked hard.)

"You just look young for your age."

(Not only the youngest stuntman but the youngest broker as well.)

One of two potential buyers straggled in. Stan's mother went through her pitch. Congenially, she led the buyers around the first floor, the upstairs and back to the living room.

After showing the house to a neighbor from next door and a dispirited couple who said not one word during the entire tour, Stan's mother told him: "You have to contend with lookee-loos. The broker's curse."

"I thought that was escrow," Stan said.

"There are many curses in the real estate business," his mother said.

There was one bright spot in the afternoon of that open house. "I'd take it," a man bald in the center with pig tail in the back said after completing a turn around the downstairs. He had a big belly which he thrust forward. "But you'll have to cut your commission in half. Tell the seller I'll give him 125 and not to bother countering. That's my offer."

Stan watched from the corner. His mother kept smiling through this, the smile she used when his father called to say he was working late (again), had to take clients out for dinner (but his mother wasn't invited), would spend the night at the club, had to go out of town (on extremely short notice), was entertaining possible financiers (at an unnamed hotel), had to interview a Finnish model who might be perfect for the part of Britomart in his proposed remake of Spencer's *Faerie Queene* ("The beauty of Britomart was her hidden identity" [yes, that, and the perfect metaphor for things he shouldn't know]).

The balding man turned out to be using the tactics of Wayne Johnson's Buy Real Estate For Nothing course, one of the many late-night infomercials running on cable. "And screw the broker," Stan's mother said.

(There were many curses in the real estate business.)

His father had similar difficulties trying to resurrect the most important work of his life: The Britomart project in turn-around, again, for the third time.

"It's the damn economy," his father said (perhaps unwilling to admit that a costume drama where the main character is a personification allegory for Chastity might be less than attractive to a studio executive who—if they remembered the story at all—did so as one of the texts they had to slog through in a Freshman survey course not too many years before).

His father tended to blame everything on the economy. If the morning paper didn't arrive or the mail was late, it was the economy. If the signal on the satellite dish wavered, it was the economy. When the neighborhood experienced a series of short blackouts each morning for three weeks running, it was the economy.

"And the studio system," his father said. "When a new regime sweeps in they sweep everything old out. They don't want to be tarred by the old brushes. They want to put their stamp on things."

Stuntmen didn't worry about projects in turnaround or houses in the Valley (or the economy). Stuntmen worried about wind velocity and air pressure in the jump bag. Though leaping off the roof onto old mattresses didn't require such precise calculations, this, too, was how Buck Simms might have started.

Stan had traversed the neighborhood on trash day and recovered a pile of mattresses. He hooked up an old red wagon to his bicycle, rolled up the mattress with some effort, and tied it to the wagon. The he dragged the whole contrivance home. Peddling was hard work with two hills to surmount before his house, and the wagon constantly threatened to tip him over and throw him onto the pavement.

Sometimes Bradley was there to help him drag each mattress off the wagon and, with a series of kicks and pulls and pushes, maneuver them by the side of the garage—out of sight of his parents. (As if they cared.) He tore up his hands the first time, tried to hide the damage, but didn't need to (they weren't watching him). Except for cursorily making sure he got to his lessons and to school, his parents seemed too busy with themselves. His father might ask Stan how his day was but before receiving an answer launch into another complaint about the economy and then about a development executive who kept him waiting over an hour only to cancel the meeting while Stan's father languished in the reception area. (The nerve.) His mother was being pressured by the woman who ran the brokerage to improve performance or "changes may have to be made." They saw each other running in or running out, a piece of toast in the mouth, a briefcase in the hand, gnawing on half a sandwich, books under the arm, a car-cup of coffee steaming through its tiny vent. Stan found he was out of socks and underwear and, after wearing the same pair for a week, began doing his own laundry. His father did take him aside and tell him that karate had to be suspended for awhile.

(What was the appropriate response to this pronouncement? Extremes of anger or concern or sorrow might make his father suspicious. A lack of emotion might produce the same result.) Stan let his lower lip quiver for a second then stopped it as his father stepped closer. Stan said, "That's all right, Dad."

(Now he would have more time to train as a stuntman.)

"Don't be upset. I promise it's only for awhile. A little while."

"Okay."

"You really liked karate."

"It's only for awhile. That's what you said."

"I promise you you'll get back to it. And we haven't forgotten your party. We need to work out the details. Maybe something small? A family party?"

Stan nodded, his father drifted off, Stan went outside to the garage where his father had a weight set, a heavy-bag, and an old stationary bike. The equipment had not been used since Stan's birth but, except for being dusty and all the iron parts covered with a scale of rust, things worked fine.

Using the exercises in the book, Stan lifted weights, repeating the same exercise over and over. There was no mention of a heavy bag and Stan was unsure if boxing skills were required. He rode the stationary bike but it squeaked. Even after the application of oil to all visible moving parts, the machine still let off a shrill noise whenever he peddled fast. Stan decided that riding outside was a better idea and substituted laps around the block for mileage on the machine. He did leg exercises, arm exercises, back work, chest, shoulders and he concentrated too, on his calves and forearms. Areas often neglected, the book said, but vital for the stuntman's ability to jump and climb, to leap and roll.

The movie station replayed the special which Stan carefully taped, and this time they made a special offer: For $29.95 they had available in limited quantities a book authored by Buck Simms (as told to H. Jaglom) on the art of the stuntman. The station would take checks if he sent in right away. Along with their philosophy of open discussion, his parents also allowed Stan to manage whatever limited money he saved. He had control over his own savings account. He pedaled to his bank, had a cashier's check made out for the amount, went to the post office and mailed away. The book arrived two weeks later.

Many of the same exercises were contained but there was a whole regimen for training much more extensive and detailed than in the book he got from the library. In the fourth week Stan took a practice jump. He exercised caution though, landing in a seated position—like Buck's book said—rolling back, slapping the mattresses with both palms, exhaling sharply. Shock Dissipation it was called.

He stood on the edge of the roof and worked on his balance. Control. The landing site seemed a long way away. In the moment before his first jump he remembered a time the year before when both his parents stayed home from concern over nearby brushfires. Santa Annas rushed off the desert pushing to the sea, giving the skies a rare clarity, a luminance in the drying. The sun was hesitant that morning. Smoke lay over the city in a bitter pall. They said the forests were burning. He was on the roof then impact, a jarring that spread out throughout his body. No breaks. No sprains. (Amazing.)

"Amazing," said Bradley.

Stan rode his bike up and down hills to strengthen his legs and develop his wind. In his driveway, he tried holding the bike absolutely still and upright to test and improve his balance.

"You're getting better at that," Bradley said.

He was up to three seconds now. He had started at nothing. He helped the gardener lift the mowers off the back of the truck, carry fertilizer bags to the backyard, rake and bag leaves.

"What are you doing, young man?" his mother said.

"Practicing the doctrine of equal political, economic, and legal rights for all human beings," Stan said. "Like you did in college, right?"

His mother had no answer for this and Stan went on working. His parents' arguments escalated. The family had not sat down together for a meal in more than a month. The maid stopped showing up and there was no explanation for her sudden and continuing absence. The house went undusted. (And the party, there was no mention of the birthday party. Was he being selfish? Trouble in the family and he focused on his party?) Dishes frequently piled up in the sink which Stan found himself washing. Trash piled up as well which Stan took out if only to stop the bad smells that came from the barrel. The pool went untended, leaves covering its surface and Stan couldn't risk swimming. Finally the gardener stopped coming as well, the grass growing out in the front yard, yellowing then dying off in patches.

No explanations were offered. But the training went on. Stan tried a new landing surface: cardboard boxes lashed together with a tarpaulin over them. He read that in the book. When he hit, the air was forced from the boxes cushioning his fall but they were only good for one landing. Unable to maintain a constant supply of boxes, he had to go back to the mattresses which limited the heights he could try. Modern stuntmen used jump bags, rubberized canvas inflated with compressed air. Like landing on a giant pillow. Maybe camping air mattresses would do.

Stan's strength and endurance increased, visibly. Wearing only a pair of briefs, he stood in the full-length mirror in his bedroom and examined his body. Muscles had developed all over. There were also black and blue bruises on his upper legs and on his arms. Stunts took hard work. He banged his head on the garage wall after too tentative a jump. He scraped his leg on the gravel when he came off the mattresses. That jump was too enthusiastic in compensation for the tentative one before.

He watched the tape he made of the Buck special. He read Buck's book. He brought the other two back to the library. They were not nearly as informative as Buck's.

In Buck's most famous stunt he leaped from the top of a water tower into a moving hay cart, one take in a master shot. Stan's father had long ago taught him terminology in case he might be interested in writing a script (though pursuing a career as a screenwriter was not recommended [because the writer is always getting screwed]), so at the least he'd be able to understand his father's scripts and give an opinion. The camera was set far enough away to view the tower from top to bottom all in the frame. In the documentary, they had slowed the shot down and Stan wasn't sure if that's how it appeared in the original film. Buck's body plummeted for what seemed like the longest time. He wore all black and stood out in good contrast against the white water tower and the light colored straw. It was funny, really, Buck landing nearly in a seated position in the hay cart, immediately swallowed up by the straw, loose bunches flying out on all sides strewing the road. The slow moving cart bounced a bit on impact then settled down, rolled out of frame.

Stan wanted to recreate that stunt but where in Los Angeles would he find a water tower and a hay cart? He knew from the history book that the gigantic airbags modern stuntmen used to cushion their fall limited the scope of the shot. No way could the camera be set blocks away to capture a fall in one take on a master. They got the fall part of the way down the building and then the aftermath. Sometimes not even the aftermath if it was too gory. Or they found a location where the fall would be covered by a slight rise in front of the camera. The stunt gave the illusion of a complete fall in one take without the finish, implying through sound effects that the body had landed. (Illusion all around—everything in life seemed to have its own metaphor for lying.)

Buck believed in safety but safety had to be balanced against the stunt and the needs of excitement for the picture. Tough, with apparently a high threshold for pain, Buck performed stunts no one would get near these days what with the potential for million dollar lawsuits. Stan mentioned something in passing to his father who said, "Insurance is killing everyone. Looks like I'm going to have to have Britomart digitally walk through fire during the rescue in the last scene. That pushed the budget up another mil."

Buck Simms would have walked through fire, put on asbestos and a wool undersuit. Leapt through the inferno and kept on going right at the camera. Britomart was a woman masquerading as a knight. Because she hid beneath knight's armor, they could use a stuntman for the gags. Put the visor down and pass through fire. On the far side the actress returns, sweeps off her helmet and shakes out her long blonde hair, black smoke and fire behind. Buck Simms would have got the stunt in one take. Beautiful. On time. On budget.

Stan knew he was not yet ready but he was determined to design his own stunt and get it in one take with Bradley's home video camera. A leap off a hotel or apartment balcony into a pool might be the way to go, no airbag required. It had been done before but the one take master made all the difference. They always stopped before they hit the pool. Not Stan. He'd go all the way. (The way Buck Simms would have done the stunt.)

He needed experience going into water from a height. Jumping off the neighbors one-meter board—a springy plank that bent down nearly to the water with only Stan's weight upon it—wasn't going to do it.

"You must know someone, Dad," Stan said.

"Why the sudden interest in diving?"

"I want to know."

Stan used guilt after his father cancelled the fifth of their "special time" meetings. Reluctantly (it seemed), his father made a few calls and then took him down to the old diving center at Pomona College, his father's *alma mater*. "I hope this makes up for the cancellations but I want you to know I'm taking time off from work to do this with you," he said.

"Thank you," said Stan.

The building was old and dark and dank and smelled of chlorine and something else. Stan couldn't identify it but it was bad. In the locker room he donned a pair of nylon shorts that he used for swimming. None of those little Speedos for him. In the cool air goosebumps rose on his arms and legs. He wrapped a towel around his body and went out to the diving pool.

Practice had just finished for the team and a group of divers came toward him. They were tall and muscular, bodies without body fat. They laughed and passed him.

His father was talking to a man dressed in a warm-up suit.

"Coach Hendry," the man said. "Your father was one of my students. I bet you didn't know that. Flunked swimming three times. Almost kept him from graduating but we pulled him through. Your father tells me you want to learn how to dive."

"I want to jump off the high board and see how it feels."

"You don't want to learn to dive, Stan?" his father said. "I thought you wanted to learn how to dive. That's why I did this for you. So you could learn how to dive."

Stan shook his head. "I want to jump."

The adults looked at each other in confusion.

Stan said quickly, "It's for your movie."

"There's no water in my movie."

"In the ocean scene. But I can tell you about that later."

"You've been thinking about my movie?

(Was everyone this easy to manipulate? He, too, was caught up in the lying.)

"Coach," his father said, "sorry about the false pretenses but can he jump?"

The coach looked at his watch. "I made the time. Go straight in, Stan. Put your hands by your sides. Think about slicing the water. We use metaphors on the diving team. Think about cutting that water like the point of a knife."

Stan took three jumps on the low board. The board was stiffer than the neighbor's propelling him up higher, out farther over the water. Jumping off the roof still had proven far more difficult. Here, the water cushioned him.

"You sure you don't want to dive," his father said, his voice booming off the tiles.

"Jump. I'm jumping," Stan said, climbing from the pool to drip water on the floor. He went to the next higher board.

"He's jumping," his father said.

Stan tried the three-meter board. He walked to the end, took a small hop and flew into space. He remembered an afternoon at the beach a year before, maybe two, late when the wind fell off and five gulls landed beside them. The surge of each new wave carried the birds higher up the sand in search of drier ground. Stan and parents sat in a depression culled and drawn by the weight of their bodies facing out toward the sea. In that moment they were then a family as the sky bled carmine at its farthest edge. The impact with the water was sharper. He went in deeper, took longer to get back to the surface, needing three kicks.

"I want the higher board," Stan said. "The really high one."

His father looked (uneasily it seemed) at the coach. Stan came over dripping water on the tile. (His father no doubt thought of danger, insurance, how much time this was all taking.) In the slight chill of the room Stan rolled his shoulders in and hunched his body for warmth.

"I can do it," Stan said. "I just have to keep my body straight and relaxed."

His father looked at the coach. The coach looked at his father. Both men looked at Stan.

"I can," he said.

Coach Hendry called over an assistant who had been sitting in the stands. "Get me an insurance waiver," he said.

The television commentators said the best divers saw the water the moment before impact. Even after spinning three times, twisting and piking they saw the water. At 180 feet per second per second time slowed down. Gravity loosed its boundaries, released them to complete their turn and spike the water knife-like without splash. The great divers saw the water. A second and half. Worlds suspended.

Stan climbed. Wide steps covered in abrasive. His footing was sure, the pool visible in the space between stairs. The floor got farther and farther away. Perhaps he was making a mistake. A thinning spot had developed on the top of his father's head. (Perhaps this jumping was a mistake. He was not ready, had not sufficiently practiced.) The pattern of the tiled floor grew indistinct.

He reached the top of the tower and kept walking. The sides were blue, the surface of the platform rough. He kept walking to the end of the platform, did not look down, kept walking and then he was in space. He remembered that in autumn, the leaves don't change in Los Angeles. Except on one small patch of road whose name he could never remember.

"You were a real pro up there," his father said.

"I'd like to try this again sometime," Stan said.

"Just jumping?" the coached asked. "You really don't want to dive? Sure. Mitch, bring him around anytime. Maybe we'll get you up there too—to learn how to jump."

He had only to find a hotel for his stunt.

He rode to one on the boulevard and discovered that, if challenged by security or hotel personnel, all he had to do was say his parents were guests in the hotel and they left him unbothered. "What room?" an overambitious assistant manager demanded the next time.

"517," Stan said. Every hotel had a 517. Stan had learned from his parents something to the effect that certainty perceived was certainty achieved. (Another illusion revealed itself.) The way he understood it was adults left children alone if the children seemed to have a purpose or a destination given to them by parents and other authority figures provided the children responded with assurance and no hesitation. "We're staying in room 517," Stan said.

"Okay," said the assistant manager. "Are you enjoying your stay?"

(He was having a fine "stay.") Stan went out by the pool.

He had to find a hotel with rooms that had patios and balconies overlooking the pool. He needed the courtyard to be small so that there wasn't much deck between the building and the pool. If he was going to jump he would only be able to get out a few feet from the railing and didn't want to miss the water. He also needed to be near the deep end. On his fifth try, he thought he found the place when he realized that the deep end faced out and away from the horse-shoe shaped building. He would manage the leap only to land in three feet of water. Nearly as bad as landing on the deck.

The search went on. His training went on. Hard to fit in all the work and at the same time find a hotel. He consulted the Yellow Pages, rode up and down the wide boulevards of the San Fernando Valley looking for the right place.

The Valley Meridian was it, the building constructed in a circle around the pool, each wall equidistant from the pool. He paced them off. Ten floors high on all sides. He prowled the hallways and figured out the perfect room. 1034. A pool facing room and thus a bit more expensive than the ones that faced the street. 1034.

Bradley was excited to hear what Stan described. "I could have helped you find the place," he said.

"You know you can't tell anyone."

"This is very exciting."

"You're only going to get one take," Stan said. "You'll have to figure out a camera angle and a move. Personally, I think you should get back as far as possible and keep a master shot but if you want to follow me down, that's okay."

They visited the hotel and Bradley took notes. Though he had in the past taped Stan leaping from the roof, he planned now, fervidly. They tried different angles, Bradley went up on the roof with Stan. Bradley stood across the yard in a long shot. Bradley placed his camera on the ground looking up as Stan leaped. Stan held the camera once and leaped with it. That jump hurt because he wasn't able to use the full shock dissipation technique without injuring the camera. Later, they edited the sequence together and watched with great excitement.

"It looks believable," Stan said.

Bradley was critical of the lighting, his own camera movement, the lack of steadiness to the frame, continuity. Then he said, "For the big one, we need to have more than one camera if you're only going to do one take into the pool."

"We can't," Stan said. "We're sneaking in."

Bradley said, "I know a whole bunch of kids who have cameras. It's like a club. They want to go into the movies."

"The hotel people don't say anything when it's just me, but ten or fifteen kids roaming around the hotel with cameras." (How would they explain that? They'd have to get more than one room, take up several positions.) "We'll never pull it off," Stan said. "Everyone has to get down there at the right time on the right day. We'd have to have a camera plot and full directions. This is turning into a production." Stan ticked off a half dozen more obstacles including the impossibility of getting ten or fifteen kids together for any reason other than a party.

"What about your birthday party?" Bradley said. "When is your birthday, anyway?"

When Stan's piano lessons came to an abrupt end as did his tutoring lessons he saw an opportunity. The arguments between his parents stopped as well. They had taken to sleeping in separate bedrooms when his father slept at home, which seemed to be less and less. One afternoon Stan waited for his mother to drive him for piano and she didn't show. Later that she night he asked her what had happened.

"I told you that we had to stop them."

They were in the kitchen eating dinner. Tofu ravioli. An acquired taste.

"You didn't say anything. I waited," Stan said.

"You're not listening. Your father and I told you."

There was a noise from the front door, keys and the door opening. Footsteps, the dropping of a heavy object onto the floor. A curse.

"Your father told you."

"Only about the karate."

His father walked in and got a beer from the refrigerator. He held it to his forehead. "How's everyone?" he said.

"I told Stan about his lessons," his mother said.

"Changes have to be made, Stan. Temporary changes we hope. How do you feel about that?"

(Certainty perceived—certainty achieved.) He said: "Like the maid and the pool cleaner and the gardener. How about someone else taking out the trash? None of my friends wash their own clothes."

Stan ran from the room. (Perhaps he had gone too far, said too much. His training was going so well and without interference from his parents. He had modified the landing surface using air mattresses taped together on top of the regular mattresses. So much easier to land.)

In a little while his father came up to his room. "I know this is hard, Stan."

"Are you getting a divorce? I see what's going on."

"Your mother and I have always said you were very observant, Stan. Very intelligent, too. You have insight. I know these changes aren't easy. We probably are getting divorced. We'll have to sell the house and move. I don't know where."

"Then I want something," Stan said, "since you've taken everything else away. You keep saying I'm going to have a party for my birthday. I've found a place. A pool party. At the Valley Meridian. I'll have a few friends. Rent a room so we can change. Can you still afford that? A cake and some drinks. We don't need a whole lunch. On the Saturday before my birthday. That's what I want. You don't even have to get me anything, else. The party will be fine."

His father, after a short consultation with his mother with Stan not present nor invited to be present (the 60s not everything they apparently claimed to be), agreed.

No one was swimming and they all had videocameras. Stan's parents asked when they were going to go in.

"We're working on something," Stan said. "A birthday video."

His parents retreated to a pair of chaise lounges. They drank ice tea. They did not let their chairs touch.

Stan had rented the room, contacted the hotel and made arrangements. Without telling his father, he had actually rented two rooms, used a borrowed (with permission) credit card. The rooms were at opposite sides of the circular building, both on the tenth floor. Stan had sworn everyone to secrecy. "Because if you say anything about the other room it'll blow it. Blow the whole thing."

They huddled around tables with amazingly sophisticated maps of the hotel grounds. Though Stan was the stuntman, Bradley acted as the unit director, whispering to the other boys, pointing out camera emplacements.

"One take," Bradley said. "That's all we get. Make sure you have fresh batteries and tape. Keep those cameras away from the water. Synchronize watches."

Stan leaned against the balcony railing of the tenth floor room selected for its strategic location to the pool. He leaned against the metal railing heated by the sun and looked out at the mountains in the distance, a layer of smog banding them. The cameras were in place, already rolling. His parents sat below. The pool shimmered.

He stepped over the railing and stood on the ledge outside, holding onto the metal behind him. The blue water of the pool shimmered below. The cameras rolled. Now his parents saw, got to their feet, and pointed, shouted. (Impossible to hear from this distance.) Cars pulled up along the street. People walked by the hotel. A slight breeze blew.

He let go of the rail and his balance changed. In that interval poised on the ledge he remembered the one winter his parents took him back east. High up the esca, he stood beside a single pine the world white around him, untracked except for the path of his footprints leading ever upward. The wind sang through the green limbs shaking out the powder like dust. He was younger then in his heavy boots, knowing little more than the anticipation of speed to come, the sharp decline. And then he leaped upon his sled, the blond wood slats receiving him, red runners slick and ready. He dropped down the hill, miles from home, flying, flying.

About the Author

IAN RANDALL WILSON's short stories and poetry have appeared in many journals including *The New Mexico Humanities Review*, *The Alaska Quarterly Review*, *The Mid-American Review*, and the *North American Review*. He is on the faculty at the UCLA Extension and lives in Los Angeles.

Acknowledgements

Many thanks to Ronald Alexander and Chuck Rosenthal for their support and critical readings. Thanks, also, to the editors of the journals in which many of these stories first appeared:

AugustCutter.com: "Absolute Knowledge"
The Boston Literary Review: "Connecting"
Eclectica: "Sometimes Rest Is Always Good"
North American Review: "Three Strikes People"
                                        "In the Space Between Stairs"
Salt River Review: "Of All Possible Rigidity" (published as "Restocking")
Tatlin's Tower: "I Am For My Nose Known"
Temenos Magazine: "The Three Bears: A Retelling"